A KILL
TONTO

Mat Fallon had stoppe
staging post to ease his
again – ahead of the men who hunted him. But a
killer he knew to be Harn Faber was there too. And
when Faber gunned down unarmed Wyatt Marsden
in front of his own daughter, who tried to avenge
him, Fallon was forced to buy in.

Little did Fallon know then, that the killing would
lead him into a web of death and intrigue, with
many old scores to be settled.

A Killing at Tonto Springs

ELLIOT LONG

A Black Horse Western

ROBERT HALE · LONDON

ISBN 0 7090 4693 6

Robert Hale Limited
Clerkenwell House
Clerkenwell Green
London EC1R 0HT

Photoset in North Wales by
Derek Doyle & Associates, Mold, Clwyd.
Printed and bound in Great Britain by
WBC Print Ltd, and WBC Bookbinders Ltd,
Bridgend, Glamorgan.

To Nesta and David, two dear grandchildren

ONE

Mat Fallon could see the Tonto Springs staging post now, sitting like a toad on the flat plain that spread immensely away from the blue bulk of mountains behind him.

He'd followed the stage road – which cut a cheese-yellow path across the dry, shimmering land – since finding it early this morning.

Now he was glad the sun was past its hottest and was westering towards the seemingly endless, undulating, occasionally tree-studded plain, heaving in the heat, before it ran slap-bang into some small, bubble-like hills maybe fifty miles away.

The trees surrounding the post rustled dryly above him as he rode into their shade, the restless breeze stirring them.

He drew rein and dismounted, gratefully stretching his six-feet-tall, well proportioned frame while allowing his grey stare to search his surroundings cautiously.

Satisfied there was no immediate danger here he worked the stiffness out of his knees. Feeling loosened now, he led the bay he rode to drink at the trough built into the corral and studied the six strong coach-horses in it warily. They stood lethargic in the dappled shade of the big cottonwood at the corral's farthest corner.

With narrow eyes that revealed nothing, Fallon's probing gaze found the barn at the back of the post now. Purposely he headed towards it.

In the shade of the trees he tied the big horse to a nearby rail and forked it a liberal amount of hay, then left it chewing gratefully, while tossing its head in an attempt to keep off the pestering flies.

He gave the five horses at the tie-rail before the staging post his close scrutiny now. One was a particularly good animal, he noted, and the saddle on it was made of fine leather. The other four were clearly unkempt cow ponies, wearing hard-used range saddles.

Satisfied there was no danger here, unless the men that followed him had changed horses, he entered the low, uninviting abode building.

It took some moments for his eyes to get used to the gloomy interior, then his gaze took in the four men sitting playing cards at a table near the glassless window, the shutters to which were wide open. At the bar, a tall man stood sipping beer.

Knowing now the danger that stalked him didn't dwell here Fallon turned his attention to the tall, thin, perspiring keeper behind the counter. He was obviously from across the border.

'*Señor?*' the Mexican enquired, his brown gaze indifferent as it stared at him.

'Beer,' Fallon said, his voice dry. He sniffed the air now. Sweet aromas of meat, vegetables and herbs all stewing together were there. 'Is that hash I smell?'

The Mexican nodded, affably enough. '*Si*.'

'A plate of that, too,' Fallon requested.

The Mexican wiped his hands on the dirty white apron around his narrow waist and turned to the fat squaw who had now appeared at the bead curtain leading to the rear of the post. He rapped orders to her in a lingo Fallon was not familiar with.

The squaw moved backwards, out of sight. Soon Fallon heard pots rattling.

He said then, eyeing the barkeep, 'I took a fork of hay for my horse ...'

The Mexican wiped a glass. 'The Company asks fifty cents for hay, *señor*. Expensive to cart, you understand. Together with the hash and beer, the charge ees a dollar.'

Fallon set his hard, weather-beaten face at that and glared with keen grey eyes, before reluctantly tossing the price on the plank bar.

'Damn it, that's a high price.'

The Mexican shrugged and took the money unemotionally, saying, 'I do not feex the prices, *señor*.'

Still a little disgruntled, Fallon moved away from the bar. He pulled out the rickety chair, drawn up under a barrel with three plain boards nailed to the top of it, and settled down to wait for his drink and meal.

It wasn't long before the squaw waddled in.

Fallon looked into her face. Definitely Indian, her flat features round and expressionless. What tribe she belonged to was anybody's guess, but judging by the silver conchos decorating the belt around the dark material of her dress: maybe Apache, or Navajo ...?

'*Gracias*,' he said.

The squaw bobbed her head almost imperceptibly, her coal-black, glittering eyes avoiding his as she retreated quickly.

Fallon ate hungrily, aware of the constant hum of insects in the air. Every now and again a swell of guffaws or curses came from the waddies playing cards. Meanwhile, the man at the bar just stood and sipped beer sparingly, his black gaze touching Fallon only once. But the stare was long and hard and made Fallon tighten up, and caused his senses to become alert to the menace in it.

After the man's brief perusal, Fallon unobtrusively studied him. He knew him now. Harn Faber – Wade Coleman's gunsel from the Cayton Town days. And he felt sure the killer hadn't recognised him.

Faber still wore his mourning-black, well cut broadcloth suit, black string tie and wide-brimmed black stetson like a uniform. And it all spoke of death. His face was sallow, thin. But the eyes: the eyes most of all. Dead, dark pools, utterly without feeling, or pity. And it prompted the question in Fallon: what was a killer like Faber doing at this God-forsaken stage post in the middle of nowhere?

Even as the thought nagged at his mind, Fallon heard the sound of iron-rimmed wheels outside grinding to a halt on the hard, worn ground. Then a female voice calling soothingly – to the horse? It distracted Fallon's attention away from the man at the bar.

He had his spoon poised half-way to his mouth when the form of the girl blocked out the bright light spearing in through the open frame of the door moments later. He was impressed with the proud way she walked, her trim body erect in the worn Levi's and red silk blouse she wore.

Fallon figured her to be about five feet five inches in height. Her raven-black hair hung down to the middle of her back from under her brown stetson. And her dark eyes flashed behind their long-lashed lids. At the provocative curve of her right hip was a holstered Colt forty-five. And, Fallon observed immediately, it looked used, not an ornament. He brought his spoon fully to his waiting mouth.

As he chewed he became aware that her luminous, dark eyes were studying him boldly and he held her gaze as it turned to one of intrigued curiosity. It didn't flinch, or drop away self-consciously, like some ladies' gazes he had known would have done.

The response from the table the rangemen sat at broke the moment.

'Wowheee!' somebody bawled. 'Howdy, Miss Jane. You sure is a sight fer sore eyes!'

Miss Jane? For some reason Fallon found his

thoughts pouncing on the piece of information. In response to the joyous call from the waddies the girl turned her gaze away from Fallon's look and smiled at the hailing cowboys.

'Hello, boys,' she called. 'Does Mace know you're in here drinking the day away?' Her voice had a bantering, teasing tone.

'You ain't goin' to tell, air you, Miss Marsden?' another puncher demanded warily. 'We's supposed to be chasin' beeves, but we found none to chase. Clean as a whistle over in the brakes, though the crick still has water in it. You'd think there'd have been some beeves foragin' about in there, now wouldn't you?'

Fallon watched the frown cloud Jane Marsden's brow; watched her hip-sway over to the crew and sit down in the chair close to the card table.

'I saw maybe a hundred head down there – oh, not three weeks since,' she said, puzzlement now clear in her voice. 'In fact, we discussed it amongst ourselves back at the Lazy M; wondered when Mace Readon was goin' to chivvy them out of there for brandin'.'

'The hell you say,' was the incredulous consensus of opinion from the card table. 'Goshdarnit, where they gone?'

Fallon ate quietly, half interested in this intriguing local mystery.

'Search me, boys,' Jane Marsden said. Fallon watched the enquiring look come to her pretty face as she stared at the riders. 'Rustlers, maybe?' she ventured.

Serious doubt immediately became apparent amongst the hands. 'Naw – we ain't had thet kind of trouble on the range fer quite a spell,' a wiry, grey-haired rangeman said. He spat fiercely into the brass cuspidor placed conveniently nearby. 'Why,' he growled, 'it must be five years since the High Baldy and the Lazy M combined to rid the range of those varmints. Five years. They sure got the message then, that this range was bad news.'

Jane Marsden shrugged, lost her doubting look. 'Well, maybe they'll turn up somewhere,' she said brightly. She rose and crossed to the bar. 'Got any limes pressed, Emilio?'

'*Si*,' the barkeep said. 'For the stage passengers when they arrive. Twenty cents to you, *Señorita* Marsden.' The Mexican turned his head and called, 'Esperanza?'

Again the squaw came to the bead curtain. Again the Mexican spoke in guttural tones. The squaw disappeared.

'The stage is late, Emilio,' Jane Marsden stated.

The Mexican shrugged. 'Eet is seldom early,' he agreed. As if to change an old subject he said, 'You here to meet your father, *señorita*?'

'Yes.'

Fallon watched Jane Marsden study the Mexican with quizzical, dark eyes now. 'About the cattle in the brakes, Emilio,' she said, 'have you seen anything suspicious?' She made a quick gesture with her left hand. 'Strange riders … cattle being moved?'

Emilio's swarthy face remained unemotional as

he returned her questioning look.

'Ten days ago I notice seex riders,' he offered. 'They spent the best part of the day working the cattle out of the brakes. When they finally got them all out, they took them south.' He added glumly, looking at Jane, 'They did not call here.'

Alerting Fallon again Jane Marsden let out a cry of what could only be astonished anger, and turned to the rangemen. 'You hear that, boys?' she demanded incredulously.

The news had obviously shocked the range hands, too. Fallon watched as they rose to a man, their chairs scraping back on the earth floor. 'Dammit, we ain't had thet kind of trouble in a coon's age,' a tall waddy growled. He turned to the barkeep. 'Hell – why didn't you say, Emilio?'

'You never ask,' came the Mexican's excuse.

'Thet ain't a damned reason,' a waddy exclaimed irately.

'I not make eet one,' snapped back Emilio. 'I thought eet was the High Baldy moving cattle. If I'm not asked, I mind my own beesiness.'

The squaw came in with the lime juice and Jane Marsden thanked her and drank thirstily.

Before any more conversation could be overheard, Fallon heard the grinding roll of wheels outside, and the cry of what had to be the stagecoach driver calling the team to a halt.

As if given some unseen signal the cowhands and Jane Marsden surged towards the door, followed by Emilio. They were swallowed up by the brilliant light of the afternoon sun coming in through the aperture.

As if he had received a signal Harn Faber stirred, drained the dregs of the beer he was drinking.

Fallon felt his gut tightening as soon as the gunslinger moved. He watched the killer slip off the tie looped over the hammer of the Smith and Wesson .38 pouched in the black leather holster at his right side. Now the gunman flipped away his long coat purposely, giving him clear, quick access to the weapon.

Fallon hardened his gaze. He found his throat had become unreasonably dry. Damn it, he thought, *what the hell is going on here*?

Then he became aware that Faber's cold, dead stare was upon him.

'I have business here, pilgrim,' the gunman said harshly. 'When it's done I'll be gone. If you're wise, you won't get brave.'

The warning was clear in his voice and eyes and Fallon immediately felt it was politic to hold his peace. He was passing through. He was in enough trouble as it was. But …

'I don't cotton to killin' in cold blood, mister,' he said harshly. 'It'd better be clean.'

Fallon met the killer's stare unflinchingly; saw it spark for a moment as he made his point. But, abruptly halting any further word-play, the group came back in through the door, minus Emilio, who, Fallon assumed, would be changing the horses.

Jane Marsden had her arm looped through the

arm of a tall, rangy man in store-bought clothes and a grey stetson, from under which long grey hair grew to touch his shoulders.

Abruptly, like a cat, Faber moved away from the bar and confronted the happy pair.

'Wyatt Marsden?' he demanded of the old man, his grim, trap-like lips hardly moving.

The tall rancher peered forward, squinting through the gloom with bright, narrowed blue eyes, set in a round, weather-worn face.

'Yes,' he said in a firm, steady voice.

A taut, deadly silence descended. Obviously seeing menace and danger here, the High Baldy waddies spread away swiftly, their hands moving to their guns. Harn Faber's cold gaze ranged over them like the swift, exploring tongue of an angry rattlesnake. With fast, sure movements he uncovered the other Smith and Wesson .38 on his left hip, and flicked the tie off the hammer.

'I don't advise you to buy in, boys,' he whispered.

Startled and, as if suddenly hypnotised by the killer's deathly, menacing voice, the High Baldy waddies moved their hands away from their pieces.

And Fallon could understand their discretion. The aura of death that surrounded Faber, he remembered, had always been intimidating. Even as the recollection flashed through Fallon's mind, the gunslinger was turning his dead eyes again towards Jane Marsden's father and without further warning, the killer's hand moved for gunmetal.

'Draw, Marsden!' he snarled.

'He's unarmed!' Jane Marsden screamed.

The exclamation galvanised Fallon, all thoughts of cold neutrality fleeing from him. From the corner of his eye, he could see Jane was going for her own gun. The sight shocked him. She stood no chance, he reasoned. It would be double murder.

His anguished eyes saw Faber was coming up with his Smith and Wesson snake-fast. Even more horrendous was the report from it, filling the staging post with sudden violent noise.

Fallon heard Wyatt Marsden's harsh cry and he saw the rancher spin round, before falling to his left.

Now Faber was turning on Jane Marsden, who had managed to get her hand on to her Colt, but not yet clear of leather. All these impressions came within the compass of micro-seconds to Fallon. But he wasn't thinking now; he was reacting instinctively. He was pulling his own Colt.

Now he was thumbing the hammer and the butt of it was thumping hard back against his palm and roaring its death-cry. Already the stage post was filling with acrid powder smoke, the noise within it head-jarring.

Fallon watched Harn Faber's tall frame spin and his cold, glittering stare rest on him, his face twisted into a demonic mask.

To Fallon's desperate surprise, Faber was levelling his gun again, even though Fallon saw blood blossoming on the gunfighter's white shirt front, near the heart. Fallon triggered again, matching the gunman.

And as Faber fired, he was mouthing words, his voice harsh and surprised, 'Taken by a fiddlefoot, damn it!'

The gunman was staring now, his evil eyes round with disbelief. But Fallon also noticed the gunsel's black, hellish gaze was already beginning to register death, as he felt the gunman's hot lead ripping through his side.

Shocked by the pain, Fallon became aware of shots to his left. One, two, three, four – their reports racketing around the gloomy stage post.

Faber was torn like a rag doll. He fell, his blood spewing out red on to the metal-hard, earth floor. And Fallon knew the High Baldy rangehands had finally, savagely, bought in on the fracas.

Watching Faber's death-throes Fallon shakily holstered his smoking Colt, then turned his attention to his wound. The lead had gone through the fleshy part of his left side. He found it was bleeding freely.

Amazed he sat down heavily on the chair he had occupied minutes ago to peacefully eat his meal. Now this, he thought. It was too damned silly for words. He should have kept his peace and ridden out; left these people to deal with their own problems in their own way.

He was clasping the wound, to try and close it up, when he became rudely aware of Jane Marsden's stark cry. He turned to look at her. She was on the floor, her hands clasped around her father's shoulders, and crying uncontrollably.

Emilio came running into the post now, carrying a nasty-looking Wells Fargo shotgun, his swarthy face alarmed. Behind him, Fallon saw one who, he assumed, was the stagecoach driver, and behind him, three passengers: two men and a well dressed woman. Their cries of horror came stark and clear in the gloom of the stage post interior.

Also, Jane Marsden's whimpers of grief were ragged and deep, searing across Fallon's confused emotions. He got up from the chair he had slumped on to and moved to her.

'Ma'am,' he grunted, attempting an apology. 'It was too sudden. I tried to get him afore he got your pa, but ...'

He was aware then of Jane Marsden's tragic, dark eyes staring up into his own, before lowering them to gaze at his wound – her look, as she did, becoming immediately round and alarmed.

Now Fallon became aware that the room seemed to be moving; that the ground under his feet seemed to be heaving like the restless waves of the sea. And he knew blood was oozing from him and if it wasn't stopped, he would be dead. He determined he had to lie down. Be still. Not move. Allow the blood to congeal.

He sat down on the floor. With an odd resentment, he thought: Dammit, I'm too young to die.

And he stared dumbly into Jane Marsden's

dark eyes as they looked down at him. Alarm filled them and she turned swiftly to the rangemen.

'Boys, we've got to do what we can.'

Fallon realised now he was shivering and he felt oddly ashamed of the fact. But also, he felt rough hands were reaching to help him.

TWO

'It should be done by now,' Wade Coleman said his tone placatory. He was seated behind the big desk in his office at the back of the High Stake Saloon. 'You worry too much, Will.'

He pulled out a stogie from the inside pocket of the well cut suit he was wearing and lit it. He was a big man – had been a powerful one – before he had allowed a more sedentary business life to soften his muscles.

He stared at the short, dour-looking man sitting in the chair across the desk from him, who returned his stare with owlish, dark eyes.

'I still don't like it,' William van Klieber said.

Wade Coleman shook his head, his heavy jaw, that had the early beginnings of jowls, quivered. 'Well, that's too damned bad,' he snorted.

'Could be,' van Klieber countered doggedly. 'I don't figure you, Wade. You could have had the Marsden spread without killin' Wyatt. The Marsden dame's taken a big shine to you.'

Wade Coleman's heavy though still handsome face broke into a disarming smile, exposing sound, strong teeth. 'An' when I've finished with the flowers and sympathy, Will,' he said reassuringly, 'she'll be putty in my hands. Believe it.'

Van Klieber remained unconvinced. 'Maybe.'

Now, as if tired of the small man's pessimism, Coleman scowled. 'Damn it,' he growled irritably, 'you know Wyatt Marsden would never have agreed to a marriage between me and Jane. He had to be removed.'

He cut the air with his big hand moodily, still glowering at the Dutchman. 'And you know I don't like uncertainties, Will,' he argued. 'And I don't like waiting. I wasted five long years in that damned penitentiary. Time to me, now, is a very precious commodity.'

His dark eyes studied van Klieber. 'I'm going to be the man around here, Will. And there'll be no foul-ups this time. This time I'll be clean.'

'Sheriff Milton is not a man to fool easily,' warned van Klieber. 'And he'll go into the matter thoroughly. Marsden – if he's dead – was a well liked and respected figure around here.'

Wade Coleman spread his arms and opened his ham-like fists. 'What would we know about a contract killing at Tonto Springs?' he demanded of his doubting friend. 'We're here, going about our normal business of running a saloon, in a normal way, for all to see.'

The Dutchman studied the man behind the desk. In the State Penitentiary Coleman's pitiless nature made him wary of him, even though the apparently genial man looking at him had befriended him.

It was strange, van Klieber reflected, Coleman's affection for him, but on more than one occasion it had proved genuine and it remained a mystery to him why it should be so. For van Klieber had to admit to himself that seldom had he come across a more coldly ruthless man, who clothed these traits in such suave and apparent caring for the human condition.

Only Wade Coleman, in van Klieber's experience, could order his own fiancee's father shot down in cold blood because he was supposedly in the way of his ambitions.

It was so stupid, too, thought van Klieber, because he knew, given time, even the untrusting and wary range-hardened Wyatt Marsden would have succumbed to Coleman's charms and the rancher would have been very useful in furthering Coleman's political ambitions, having a lot of influence in the county.

But, as Wade had said, he was a man in a hurry. And that, maybe, could be his second downfall. He could make one rash move too many and …

Van Klieber blinked, puzzled by his own feelings. What held him to this man? The excitement of being around him? Or recognising in Coleman a potential ticket to the good life? For Coleman was a shrewd and capable businessman, which van Klieber freely admitted to himself at more honest moments, he was not. And Coleman seemed to like him. No, damn it, he did like him and had demonstrated this more than once.

Yes, it was Coleman's utterly relentless quest for wealth, and the good things that went with it, that held him, plus ...

Perplexed, van Klieber sucked his thin bottom lip as the realisation came to him.

Plus, strangely, he loved the man. Was excited and stimulated by being around him. And yet, at the same time, was afraid of him.

'So, what do we do now?' he said.

'Wait for the news of Wyatt's killing to break.'

With that cold declaration, Coleman blew a cloud of smoke he had drawn from his stogie and smiled, exposing even, white teeth. 'Then, after a respectful time, lead Jane Marsden to the altar,' he continued blandly, as if totting up a balance-sheet. 'After that, find that oil under the Lazy M.'

'You're mighty sure it's under there,' said van Klieber sceptically.

'I am.' Coleman's eyes glittered behind their layers of fat. 'And I'll lay dollars it's under High Baldy, too.'

Van Klieber was still sceptical. 'What's so important about oil? This is good cattle country. And cattle's where the money is.'

Coleman chuckled quietly. 'That's where you're wrong, Will,' he said. 'I see oil as being the biggest moneymaker the world has ever known. And I aim to be in on the ground floor.'

As he spoke an urgent knocking came to the office door.

'It's open,' invited Coleman.

He saw it was Billy Mayer, the small, moon-faced barkeep at the High Stake. One of the six he employed. The keeper's blue eyes were round with excitement.

'Mr Coleman,' he said, his voice high-pitched, 'news just came in with the stage. Wyatt Marsden's been gunned down at Tonto Springs staging post. They got the killer, though. Some stranger plugged him. The opinion is the shootist was a hired gun, not from around these parts.'

Wade Coleman got up slowly, making a great play of being apparently totally ignorant of the killing, dazed shock drawing his heavy features.

'I don't believe it,' he gasped, as if bewildered. 'Why, Wyatt hadn't an enemy in the world.'

'It's true, Mr Coleman, nevertheless,' insisted Billy gravely. 'They say Miss Marsden's inconsolable.'

As if numbed by the news, Coleman put his hand to his mouth, as though still unable to comprehend the news. 'Yes … Jane.'

He turned to van Klieber, mock horror now on his face. The Dutchman was impressed anew with his friend's superb acting.

'I must go to her, Will – immediately,' Coleman blurted, as if manfully pushing the news to the back his mind, his thoughts going out to Jane. 'The poor girl must be out of her mind with grief.'

He turned his gaze back to the barkeep. 'Billy,' he ordered seriously. 'Have my horse saddled at once. I want it outside the saloon in ten minutes.'

Billy Mayer nodded. 'Sure, Mr Coleman.'

When the barkeep had gone, Coleman turned to van Klieber. Van Klieber held his now dark stare.

'So,' Coleman said, surprised. 'Harn Faber finally got careless.' Then he smiled. 'But it's worked out good, Will. There is nobody now who could stick mud on us.'

'In Harn, you've lost the services of a top gunsel,' van Klieber pointed out, feeling he should defend the killer. 'And Faber wasn't a man to spill the beans on anybody.'

Coleman nodded slowly, thoughtfully. 'Yeah, you're right, Will,' he admitted. 'But I've a feeling we won't be needing Harn's particular talents any more.' Now he grinned, gleefully. 'And too bad Harn isn't around to pick up the other half of the two thousand dollars he should have collected when the job was done.'

Van Klieber stared at his friend and a chill came anew to his backbone as he witnessed again the evil, ruthless side of Coleman's nature. Harn had been a faithful member of Coleman's clique. He wondered if his own fate would be dismissed so easily.

'Handy,' he said, with a jocularity he did not feel.

Coleman smiled at him. 'Yeah,' he agreed.

He took a deep breath. 'Well, I'm going to comfort Jane now, Will,' he announced jauntily, 'so deal with anything that comes up. Can't say when I'll be back, but this is the opportunity to make Jane feel even more warmly towards me and maybe, on the rebound from Wyatt's death ...'

Van Klieber watched Coleman's wolf-like grin spread across his face as he broke off mid-sentence, his dark, shapely brows rising triumphantly. 'Truly, old friend,' he said with a happy sigh, 'I can't visualize any problems.'

Van Klieber watched him rise from the chair and pull on his grey stetson, then felt Coleman's affectionate pat on the back as he moved to pass him. 'Don't worry, Will,' he said soothingly. 'Trust me.'

Van Klieber watched Coleman's broad, expensively suited back as he left the office and could only feel deep awe for the relentless ambition in the man, which comprehensively swamped any doubts he had about him.

* * *

Fallon figured he must have passed out, for he found himself fighting his way up through a pain-filled red mist.

Now he remembered rough hands patching him up in the stage post, then lifting him on to a buckboard.

He became aware he was in a large room and that brutal, searing agony was biting his side. A man was bending over him, sewing him up.

He couldn't help crying out, harshly. Within seconds he felt leather being forced between his lips and the order to 'Bite on thet, mister,' coming from a waddy behind him.

Bright-eyed with the hurt in his body, Fallon

looked around him. He was being held prone by
big, work-toughened hands.

He was on a table, in a big room, the walls of
which were covered with rifle-cupboards, spreads
of longhorns, Indian regalia. And heavy, Mexican-
style furniture was placed around it at well-
thought-out intervals. It was clearly a man's
room. No woman had had a hand in this.

He was bare to the waist and a tall, spare man
with an ascetic face was sewing up his wound.
Behind him was Jane Marsden. She was looking
down at him her eyes round, dark pools. Two
grim-faced waddies were sitting on a long couch
playing with their hats in their gnarled hands.

Desperately, Fallon clamped his strong teeth on
the leather to endure the savage pain stabbing at
him and he felt sweat now begin to run freely off
his forehead.

He could not help but wince against the sudden,
vicious needles of agony, sending waves of acute
discomfort flooding through every nerve end in his
body.

The austere man bending over him growled,
'Damn it, hold still.'

Fallon felt his body begin to tremble involunta-
rily. He bit harder and steeled himself against the
harrowing hurt he'd woken up to.

Like a cool splash of mountain water, he felt a
cloth dabbing his forehead and he looked up into
Jane Marsden's concerned gaze, a wet flannel in
her hand.

Then the harsh, stabbing pain stopped, melting

down to a thumping, throbbing ache pulsing from his side.

'I'm done stitching,' growled the man who had bent over him, hooked needle in hand. He stared at the men holding him down. 'Help him up.'

Fallon felt hands take him and ease him up. He couldn't help the gasp of pain breaking from him as he sat upright.

'I'm going to bandage you up now, son,' the ascetic-looking man told him.

With the information conveyed, the man – who Fallon now reckoned had to be the local sawbones – began to wrap him up.

'You'll live,' the doctor was saying. 'But keep out of the saddle for at least a week. Give it a chance to heal up. You had a nicked vein, that's why you bled so, but the wound itself isn't a serious one.'

Doubt filled Fallon. Damn it, he should be riding on.

'I've no place to stay,' he pointed out.

'You are the guest of the Lazy M until you are well enough to travel,' Jane Marsden's tired, grief-dulled voice came, though with enough firmness in it to suggest she would accept no argument, adding, 'Fact is, we could use an extra hand if you feel inclined to stay on when you've got over your wound.'

The thought came to Fallon immediately: the Lazy M could be a useful place to hole up while he healed …

'My thanks, ma'am,' he gritted, fighting his pain.

Just then a big, handsome, heavy-faced man came bustling into the large room and made straight for Jane. He looked smart in his black pinstripe suit and grey, low-crowned stetson.

The sight of him caused Fallon to stiffen. First Harn Faber, now Wade Coleman! By God, how many more surprises would the day hold?

And he was amazed to see Coleman take Jane into his arms with loving care.

'I came as soon as I heard the news,' Coleman said, adding, as if outraged. 'Who could have done such a terrible thing?'

And Fallon was amazed to see Jane melt into Coleman's big arms. Even more strange, he was appalled when she allowed him to pull her small head to his deep chest and pat it.

Fallon could now hear deep, harrowing sobs breaking from Jane. It was as though she had been teetering on the brink of tears all the time she had stood, cool cloth in hand, administering to him.

It was then Coleman's dark eyes found Fallon's stare. And it satisfied Fallon to see Coleman's gaze harden, then narrow and puzzled alarm flicker across his heavy features.

You remember me, eh, Coleman? Fallon thought as cold rage filled him. He wanted, there and then, to expose Coleman for what he was, if only to save Jane Marsden grief. But to do that, Coleman would be swift to reveal his own none too savoury past and he figured the time wasn't right for that.

So Fallon sat and watched the touching scene and held his peace, though his stomach churned to see such a lovely woman as Jane Marsden being mauled by that gut-low sidewinder.

After further embraces and soothing words from Coleman, which Fallon knew could tumble all too easily from the man's lips, Coleman, after one more icy stare in his direction, led her away, out of the room.

But just before they left, Jane paused and turned to the nearest waddy, sitting on the settee.

'See Mr Fallon is comfortable, Slim,' she said.

'Sure, Miss Jane.'

The tall, ageing rangeman came towards Fallon. 'You feel like eatin', son?' he said. 'Chow's about to be dished up.'

Before he answered, Fallon watched Coleman lead Jane out of the room, then, grunting his pain, slid gingerly from the table. As he stood up, he felt as though he was floating and it took a considerable effort of will to remain erect and in control.

'Sounds good,' he said. He studied the waddy's long, gaunt face and pale blue eyes. 'That's Wade Coleman with Miss Jane, ain't it?'

The rangeman's eyes narrowed sharply as they met his stare. 'Know him?'

Fallon nodded. 'Years ago,' he said. 'Ran a gamblin' house up-country – place called Cayton Town. They struck a seam of gold in the hills above it one time and it became one wild place for a year or two. Then it played out and, purty soon, everybody went back to cattle an' farmin', or moved on to the next strike.'

He could also have said Coleman had made big money out of cheating the gambling miners; had been deeply involved in land-grabbing there, too, though it was never proved he had any hand in the killings that went on, to enforce the heists.

The judge who had passed the sentence said he knew Coleman was black guilty of having a hand in the killings, but there was no firm proof forthcoming and Coleman had good lawyers.

Fallon fought down the ice-cold hatred in him. And he was sure in his own mind that Coleman had been behind the killing of his own father. A killing which had caused his mother to take her own life. He had found her hanging from a beam in their barn. She had left a note saying she couldn't face a life without his pa.

Fallon blinked, the hard lines setting on his face. Again he felt the raw, bitter sorrow that had assailed him then, renewing itself. Even though he'd had no hard proof Coleman had been mixed up in his father's death, he knew, and, as a raw, pimply kid, he had confronted Coleman in his own gambling-den, bent on revenge, only to be shot down from behind. He had been lucky to survive. And it had been suggested it had been Harn Faber who had done the back-shooting.

When he had healed up, hoping to return to their homestead, he'd found he hadn't one – the bank foreclosing on the farm because of debt.

Well, the first hold-up had been easy, he

recalled; the second even easier. But on the third, in his youthful exuberance, he had grown careless and his exploits earned him two years in the county jail. The only comforting thing that bad time had come up with was to learn that Coleman had been sent to prison for six years.

But now, what made this business he had butted into so puzzling, was the fact that it had been Harn Faber who had gunned down Jane's father. Faber had been Coleman's top gunsel during those murderous days …

Fallon had his startling trend of thought broken as the waddy at his side said, 'He runs the High Stake Saloon in Greenville, the big town on this range. He came here two years ago. He made a play for Miss Jane right off. He has a tongue smooth as cream.'

Fallon nodded. 'Yeah,' he said absently. 'That's Wade Coleman.'

And immediately, Fallon knew he had to stay on this range, if only to find out what Coleman was doing here. And to hell with the Mather brothers trailing behind him.

* * *

Sitting on the sofa in the small, private room off the big lounge, Jane Marsden stared into Wade Coleman's seemingly loving and caring eyes, and she felt warm and safe in his arms. She felt thankful, even though her father had been ruthlessly gunned down less than three hours ago, that she had another protector in Wade to replace him.

'Thank you, Wade, for coming so quickly,' she said softly and rested her hand on his deep, immaculately suited chest.

'Honey ...' Wade Coleman paused a moment, as if fumbling for words. 'You already know you mean more to me than any words can say. Your grief is mine. My only thoughts are for you. You know I want to be at your side for ever.'

She felt his lips touch her forehead and she pressed to meet them, their tender caress calming her.

Then she said, 'Who could have sent that killer to do such a thing, Wade?' She whimpered, fresh tears breaking out from her dark eyes. 'And why? As far as I knew, pa hadn't an enemy in the world.'

Wade Coleman shook his head, disturbing his long, neat black hair. 'I don't know, Jane,' he said. Then he hardened his tone, 'But, by God, I'll do all in my power to get to the bottom of it, you have my word.'

Jane dropped her head, her dark, lustrous, raven hair brushing across her bowed shoulders. Her grief was plain to see. 'I feel hollow.' She sighed. 'Dead inside. I don't know what to do. Pa always looked after things ...'

She felt Wade's large hand stroking her hair and patting it.

'Honey, *I'm* here,' he said soothingly.

She felt calm comfort filling her at that assurance, despite her grief.

'Oh, Wade,' she breathed. She felt his kiss again, this time on her cheek.

'Let me do the worrying for you from now on,' he whispered soothingly. 'Allow me to take your Pa's place until ...'

Jane lifted her head from Wade's shoulder, her dark eyes searching his, her senses sharpened and anticipatory. 'Go on, Wade.'

She felt his big hand caress her cheek. 'Honey, I don't want it to appear as though I'm rushing things,' he murmured, 'because it isn't like that. For now, all I want is to be here, protecting you, comforting you. But you know it would make me the proudest man in the world to take you down the aisle and call you my bride.'

Jane sighed. She could not suppress the thrill that hurried through her.

'Oh, Wade,' she said. 'Could it be?'

'You only have to say the word, Jane,' he said softly in her ear. 'I'd invite the whole county to our wedding.'

Jane felt her heart thump against her ribs. She had never known a man like Wade Coleman. Suave, sophisticated, attentive, gentle. All she had known were rough, honest range riders; had been part of them, giving and taking with the best of them.

Then Wade had invaded her life, melting her as if she were some wobble-kneed teenager, instead of being twenty-four years of age and used to dealing with over-amorous range hands.

She had never been able to understand her Pa's

objections to Wade. It had seemed as though, from
the first moment he had met him, he had taken an
instant dislike to Wade and would not com-
promise on it. Said he had a gut feeling about him,
for all his charm.

She sighed and sank back into Wade's arms,
knowing the strength of his character and feeling
the power of his body, and immersing herself in
the warming sensations they gave her.

She felt her senses reeling with the charm of
Wade. But, annoyingly, like a silent voice in her
head, a gnawing guilt filled her, too, making her
feel as though she was betraying Pa – falling into
Wade's arms like this, so soon after he had
been …

She whimpered and fought against the pain his
death had brought.

But she needed someone to lean on and Wade
was here, giving her the love her Pa had never
been able to show her, even though she knew he
had cared for her very deeply.

'Give me some time, Wade,' she said then, hurt
by the uncertainty that had now invaded her.

She felt Wade's kiss again, on her lips this time,
and she tingled all the way down her petite,
almost perfect, body.

'We'll talk about it later,' he whispered in her
ear. 'When the pain has eased.'

She felt his lips press on hers again, thrilling
her. Then he said, 'Honey, I don't want to appear
unfeeling, but there are certain matters that have
to be attended to …'

She felt him squeeze her hands gently. She met his stare as he looked into her dark, luminous eyes. Then he said, 'After Wyatt has been interred ...'

Jane couldn't help the sudden moan of grief that escaped her and Wade was quick to hold her tenderly to his chest. She nestled into the protection of his arms while she composed herself. Then she said, 'I'm sorry, Wade. I'm being weak, silly. Please go on.'

She felt his hand brushing her hair. 'Nothing to be sorry about, honey,' he breathed. He paused, as if searching for words, before saying, 'What I was about to say is, after a decent time, maybe you would consent to be my bride.'

Jane sighed, a dream-like happiness filling her despite her grief. Wade Coleman was a dashing, handsome man; the beau lots of girls on the range would give their eye-teeth to possess. She looked into his dark, seemingly warm eyes. The words just slipped out; they didn't need thought.

'I'd be proud, Wade. Real proud.'

She felt his lips touch her forehead. 'The age difference,' he murmured. 'I *am* forty ...'

'I've never even thought about it,' she admitted. 'Does it matter?'

She heard Coleman's sigh of satisfaction and felt his arms take her afresh.

'No, Jane,' he breathed. 'It doesn't matter at all.'

* * *

Alone Mat Fallon sat on the verandah that ran the

length of the Lazy M bunkhouse, digesting his meal when Wade Coleman stepped out of the ranchhouse. Fallon saw the satisfied smile on his lips.

And Fallon's gut tightened. His grey eyes narrowed as he met Coleman's dark stare, now reaching across the bare area of ground between them. These were different eyes from the ones Jane Marsden had been looking into seconds ago. These eyes were evil.

Unable to stop his body from tensing, Fallon watched Coleman stride over to him, the saloon-owner's heavy face set hard and menacing.

'You've got a week to leave this range, Fallon,' Coleman hissed, without preliminaries, when he reached him.

Fallon met Coleman's dark stare. 'And if I don't?' he growled. 'You ain't got Harn Faber to clean up your problems now.'

Coleman's face twitched into a mirthless smile. 'A week,' he growled. 'Beyond that, you won't be a problem.'

'I reckon I ought to tell Miss Marsden about you, Coleman,' Fallon rasped, hoping to spur Coleman.

Fallon's cold threat brought Coleman's bulk craning forward full of devilish menace. He stepped on to the verandah, his eyes coals of evil, burning in their fat-lined sockets.

'You've just shortened your life-expectancy to zero, Fallon,' he breathed. 'This time there'll be no mistakes.'

With that Coleman stepped off the verandah, eased himself into the saddle of his big chestnut and rode off without a backward glance.

Fallon kept his hard gaze on the saloon owner until he was out of sight behind the barns south of the ranch. And fearsome hate filled him.

'You figure, huh, Coleman?' he said then, his eyes two chips of cold steel. 'I reckon I'll have something to say about that.'

THREE

Brink and Chance Mather came out of the mountains and urged their tired horses across the big range stretching before them.

They had to admit they had lost Fallon's trail in the mountains. Now it would be a matter of asking around until they could come up with another lead.

Chance scowled at the prospect. He was getting fed up with Brink's constant pushing. They had been on Fallon's trail three weeks now. Had it been up to him, Chance decided, he'd have dropped the search two weeks ago. Their brother James had made a fatal mistake when he had called Fallon out.

Chance remembered the consensus of opinion in town, when he had gone in to pick up James's body. It was firmly stated James had pulled on Fallon and had left Fallon no choice. And, he had been told, Fallon, disgusted that old scores still simmered, waiting to be settled on the Cayton range, had saddled up. He had drawn what pay was due to him at the Double Bar X where he worked and had headed south for a new life.

Chance blinked hard, resentful eyes. But Brink and Pa knew only two things: an eye for an eye, a tooth for a tooth as the Bible directed and to hell with turning the other cheek!

Chance growled this time, spat and shook his head and looked with slitted eyes at his brother, riding ahead of him, perched atop his sweaty roan mare. His long back and high-held shoulders were hunched forward aggressively. Brink'd keep going until hell froze over to avenge the killing of kin, Chance concluded sourly.

He cursed under his breath as he recalled that hot, bloody afternoon two weeks ago when they had caught up with Fallon, surprising him.

Fallon had not known of the family's need to avenge their own; hadn't known they had been on his trail. And the damned silliest part, Chance's thoughts now raged – it had been agreed by all the family, himself included, to face Fallon, fair and square, out of pride. Pride, damn it!

His eyes narrowed as he remembered. Fallon had reacted like a cornered cougar. It had been a brief, savage fight. Pa had been shot out of the saddle and had been dead before he had hit the ground, blood blossoming from the wound to his heart.

Chance's eyes sparkled coldly. Fallon had escaped, but not before burning a groove across Brink's right upper arm and sending himself scuttling to the rocks, his mount running hell-bent into the hills.

Burying Pa, as Brink had insisted they do there and then out of respect, had lost them valuable time, and temporarily, Fallon. There had come a chance later, though, when they had got near enough to Fallon, to try for him with Brink's Sharps rifle, the Big Fifty with the telescopic sight. It had been a very long shot. And Brink had missed. But not by much, judging by Fallon's quick disappearence.

Again Chance spat and glowered at his brother's back, recalling the missed chance. He had bluntly aired the opinion that Brink had neither the eye nor the steadiness for such a weapon. And Brink had raged at him that it took time to master such a gun. He hadn't got used to the telescopic sight yet. But one day, he'd promised fiercely, he'd make Chance eat his words.

Chance spat and glared again. It was just an expensive toy, was his candid opinion. More to the point, the miss had lost them Fallon again.

'There's gotta be a town close,' Brink muttered through dust-rimmed lips. 'And Fallon must be needin' vittles.'

'Damn it, Brink, do we have to keep doggin' him like this?' Chance spat. 'What he did, we brung upon ourselves.'

Brink's blue gaze was icy as Chance met it – almost malevolent.

'I don't want to hear such talk ever again, Chance, you hear?' he hissed. 'Fallon killed your brother James an' gunned down Pa. We'll follow him to hell, and beyond, if need be.'

Chance glowered at his brother's hard, thin face, stubbled with a week's growth of beard, but decided to hold his peace and settled back in the saddle again and stared dull-eyed at the undulating, seemingly endless range before them.

Half an hour later, they stumbled on the cheese-yellow trail cutting across the big land.

'Gotta lead to somewhere,' growled Brink sourly.

The discovery perked Chance up a little, too.

'Got to,' he agreed, visualising a long, cool beer.

Chance gee'd-up his scrawny-looking piebald and brought it alongside Brink's roan and they settled into a steady, mile-eating gait.

They could see the rider, coming in from a trail that arrowed away to the west, as a dot at first. He gradually grew larger and larger until he joined them at the meeting of the trails.

'Well, damn it,' breathed Brink, his great surprise clear on his bleak face and in his voice when he saw who it was, 'Wade Coleman! From now on, don't anybody tell me coincidence don't exist.'

Chance felt the whole of his plump body tighten up. He didn't like Wade Coleman, never had. He was a deadly, ruthless man; though, he grudgingly admitted, he'd always paid well, and, as far as he knew, had dealt square.

During the Cayton Town days, Coleman had put plenty of work the family way. Raiding gold shipments, burning out small ranchers. High paying work, but still, he didn't like him. Cunning as a rattlesnake and as deadly, was Chance's personal opinion.

He studied Wade Coleman's dark stare, that seemed to light up at the sight of them. The sun was a huge, orange ball low on the horizon behind Coleman dazzling Chance as he fought to see the saloon keeper's features clearly.

Brink reared up in the saddle and said, with a sour grin on his face and without preliminaries,

'You git out ...'

Coleman nodded. 'I got out,' he affirmed. 'One year's remission for good behaviour.'

Brink's grin faded and he growled and spat as his face went back to its normal, bitter look. 'The hell you did,' he said meanly. 'We had to do the whole damned term.'

'You were lucky they didn't hang you,' reminded Coleman.

Brink's eyes narrowed and went cold blue at that. 'I could say the same about you, Coleman,' he hissed.

'You could,' countered Coleman, 'but it's water under the bridge now.'

The saloon owner hunched his big frame forward in the saddle and he narrowed his eyes, giving his face a shrewd look. 'What's more to the point,' he said, 'what brings the Mather brothers to this neck of the woods? And where's James and your Pa? One time, your clan was never parted.'

Chance waited for Brink to speak. It was always up to his brother to say what he thought should be said about their business.

'Could ask the same about you, Coleman — about bein' in this neck of the woods, that is,' Brink countered. 'You got somethin' goin' here?'

Coleman smiled broadly and spread his big hands. 'You know me, boys ...'

'Yeah,' grunted Brink sourly. 'Sure we do. An' if we hadn't business on, we would maybe hang around awhile. But the fact is we're trailin' Mat Fallon. He kilt James an' Pa.'

Chance, his blue eyes always searching, could not help but notice the sudden alert change that came to Coleman's face and a sort of triumphant satisfaction fill it.

'That the truth?' he said quickly, warmly. 'Well, boys, seems this is a fortuitous meeting –'

'Hell, talk American,' cut in Brink.

'I mean, Brink –' Coleman looked from one to the other '– Chance – that I know where Fallon is,' he supplied. 'Maybe, for a favour, I could tell it.'

'Hell,' snorted Brink. 'From what I remember, Fallon has no love for you, nor you for him after he came to call you out. An' I recall you had Harn Faber gun down his Pa. So why haven't you dealt with him yourself?'

'I have my reasons,' Coleman said smoothly, his face betraying nothing. 'And he doesn't know for sure Harn did the killing.'

'I figure he sure as hell guessed it – otherwise he wouldn't have braced you in your own backyard.'

'Like the callow, impetuous youth he was,' smiled Coleman.

'Well,' grunted Brink, scowling and bitter, not appreciating the saloon owner's sarcasm. 'He sure as hell has growed since then. Where is he, Coleman?'

'Come to town with me, boys,' Coleman invited suddenly. 'We'll discuss it. I'm sure you'll feel more amenable with some good food, a bath and a couple of whiskies under your belts.'

'I'd rather finish it with Fallon,' grated Brink, much to Chance's chagrin. Coleman's proposition sounded much better.

'Take my word, Brink,' Coleman assured. 'Fallon isn't going anywhere for a few days. He gunned down Harn Faber and took lead in the exchange.'

A griping, unreasonable fear gripped Chance's stomach to hear that. Fallon had taken out Harn Faber? He watched Brink's stare narrow at the news, too, his thin face tighten as uncertainty filled it. 'The hell he did,' his brother breathed.

And Chance licked his thick, suddenly dry, lips. Fallon was proving to be more lethal than a bag full of diamond-backs. And this news thoroughly convinced him that to deal with Fallon safely, it would have to be a bushwhacking; no more of that nonsense about meeting him square.

* * *

The ride to Greenville had been brisk, now Chance leaned back in the easy chair in the High Stake's rear office and blew a cloud of cigar smoke.

This was the life-style he approved of. He felt
much better for a bath, a shave and a change of
clothes. Coleman had laid it all on – and the
boarding house accommodation which, he'd told
them smugly, the saloon owner also owned.

The hotel stood three storeys tall, at the better
end of the sprawling town of Greenville, which,
they'd found, nestled by a tree-shrouded lake in a
two-mile-wide hollow in the range, and couldn't be
seen until a man ran almost slap-bang into it.

Now Chance watched Brink narrow his eyes
and stare through the veils of smoke wreathing
before him at the big man behind the desk.

'You allus had style, Coleman,' he said. 'I gotta
admit to that.'

'I've got more than that, boys,' the saloon owner
said. 'A heap of business I can put your way.'

'Such as?'

'Trading beef?'

Though his attitude indicated interest, Brink
said, his mood still vicious, 'We want Fallon first.
Until he's out of the way we're in the market for
nothin'.'

Coleman pursed his lips and glanced at van
Klieber sitting silent and watchful in the corner of
the room. Coleman had introduced the Dutchman,
cleared him as one of them, when he and Brink
had objected to his presence.

'Sure, Brink,' Coleman said then, smoothly. 'I
can understand that. But, for giving you Fallon's
hide, I need a little something in return.'

Brink shook his head. 'We did six years for you,

Coleman. No promises. Give us Fallon ... then we'll talk.'

Coleman arched his brows and looked hurt. 'You didn't do those years for me, boys,' he said. 'We were all in it together. I saw you right, didn't I? I had money banked for you for when you got out?'

Chance felt he should butt in. 'Brink, we gotta admit to that,' he said, staring hopefully at his brother. 'Coleman saw us right.'

Coleman beamed and looked gratefully at Chance for his intervention. 'Thank you, Chance.'

Brink scowled. 'Nothin' we didn't earn,' he snorted unimpressed. He waved a hand impatiently. 'You lined your own pockets good, too, Coleman,' he rapped, doggedly.

'Sure I did,' Coleman countered. 'I was the brains.' He blinked and sighed and his look hardened. 'Well, if we can't do business, boys ...' he said with an air of resignation.

Chance felt he should intervene again. 'Now hold on,' he said. 'I want to hear what you have to say, Coleman.' He glowered at his brother. 'Damn it, we need work, Brink.'

'It could pay high,' Coleman slipped in persuasively.

Chance leaned his fat body forward, scowling into Brink's lean, bitter face and wary eyes before turning and addressing Coleman.

'Spill it, Wade,' he urged then. 'Take no notice of Brink, y'hear?'

Coleman smiled and seemed to relax. 'Well, the

play is rustling out the High Baldy, one of the biggest ranches on this range,' he said. His dark gaze slid from Chance to the more sceptical Brink. 'I have thirteen men in the hills already, chewing at them.'

Coleman became brisk now, businesslike, as if warming to the proposition he had.

'The deal is this. I can give you information. Cattle movements, etc. All you have to do is lift the beef and sell it. There are plenty of markets across the border in Mexico. What you make on it, you can keep. I want no cut, no involvement, apart from giving you the lowdown.'

Brink's narrow, swarthy face registered his distrust. 'You want no cut?' he rasped. 'There's got to be somethin' in it for you,' he added warily.

Coleman again narrowed his eyes and a look of angry impatience crossed his features. 'Do you want the deal?' he rapped. 'If not, leave the office and leave my hotel. I'm a busy man.'

Brink pursed his lips, clearly not impressed by Coleman's brusqueness and seemingly still not happy with Coleman's proposition. Seeing it, Chance growled, 'Damn it, Brink, you're bein' bull-headed!'

Blink ignored him. 'Why us?' he quizzed, not even looking at Chance, just keeping his steely gaze on Coleman.

Coleman's tone now became brisk and sincere. 'Because I've worked with you, tested you, and can trust you not to involve me if it goes wrong for you.'

Brink took a lungful of smoke knowing the explanation to be the truth, and not flattery.

'Where's Fallon?' he grunted now.

Coleman's heavy features were enquiring. 'Do we have a deal?' he demanded, his voice hard.

Chance watched for his brother's reaction apprehensively. At length, Brink nodded and said,

'You got a deal, Coleman. Now … give us Fallon."

Coleman smiled and leaned back in his leather chair. 'Pour the boys a glass of the good stuff, Will,' he told van Klieber. Then his dark eyes met first Chance's stare, then Brink's.

'Fallon is at the Lazy M ten miles out of town,' he said. 'I can maybe even lure him out for you, boys. Meantime, all you need to do is enjoy my hospitality.'

Chance looked happily at Brink and Brink even managed a quick smile.

'Nice to do business with you again, Wade,' Brink said and sipped the bourbon van Klieber handed to him.

*   *   *

For three days Mat Fallon brooded over whether or not to warn Jane Marsden about Wade Coleman.

Coleman had hardly ever been away from the ranch and was always at Jane's side. Attentive, affectionate, gentle. And it was obvious Jane had fallen for his charms hook, line and sinker; a fact which riled Fallon even more. Damn it, he thought moodily, Jane had to see through him sooner or later; had to. She was too fine a lady to be tangled up with that sonofabitch.

But he'd heard that when a woman really took a shine to a man, he could do no wrong. So he hesitated, hoping for Coleman to show his wolf's hide, not the sheepskin he was wearing at the moment.

Now Fallon sat on the bunkhouse verandah, feeling stronger each morning he awoke. He figured another few days and he'd be healed up good and almost back to his full strength.

And with liver, steak and eggs for breakfast ...

He picked his teeth gratefully and felt sure it was on Jane Marsden's orders.

But now he was surprised to see her coming across the worn ground from the main ranchhouse to the bunkhouse and making straight for him – the sombre, black, ankle-length mourning gown she was wearing enhancing her petite, exciting figure.

Since she had gone out of the room with Wade Coleman the afternoon they had sewed him up, she had not been near him.

Fallon rose and touched his stetson with a horny finger.

'Mornin', ma'am.'

'Well, Mr Fallon?' she said. Though she sounded cheerful, Fallon noticed that sadness still dwelled at the back of those big, dark eyes. 'Are the boys looking after you?'

'Fine, ma'am,' he said. 'But the name is Mat.'

He was surprised to see a hint of colour tinge her cheeks. She shook back her raven hair, that shone lustrously in the early morning sun.

'Fine with me – Mat,' she said. Her dark eyes questioned him now. 'Have you thought about the job I offered you?'

Fallon nodded. 'I'll take it, ma'am,' he said.

Some of the sadness seemed to leave her at his answer, to be replaced by vague relief, though he could have been mistaken.

A hint of amusement touched her face now. 'I have a first name too, Mat,' she countered. 'It's Jane.'

He smiled. 'Touche, as Pa used to say, though I sure don't know exactly what it means.'

Jane's face lit up now, sweeping away the strained, tired look it had. 'It fits,' she said.

Then her face returned to its sad profile and the dark eyes searched him thoughtfully.

'I have to be honest with you, Mat,' she said quietly. 'I'm hiring you for your ability to use your gun, more than to haze cows. The rustling down in the brakes – you must have heard us talk about it at the stage post – and my father's death has set the whole range on edge.'

Fallon felt his gut tighten. Damn it, he should say something about Coleman – and his involvement with Harn Faber, her father's killer. But ragged doubt still dogged him. From what he'd seen of her relationship with Coleman, she'd

never believe him. He had to find some other way
to convince her.

While he wrestled silently with his indecision,
Jane said, 'We bury father this afternoon, Mat. Do
you feel strong enough to attend? It's only a short
ride from the ranch.' She turned to indicate a hill
a mile behind the ranchhouse. 'On top of there.
From that position, you can see almost all of the
Lazy M range. Pa always said, it was the only
place he could rest peaceable.'

Upon the mention of her father she paused and
blinked, and a tear rolled from her left eye. She
looked away. To Fallon, it was obvious her grief
was still great. And he had a sudden urge to take
her in his arms and hold her. But he said, softly,
'In time, the pain passes, Jane. Believe it.'

As if appreciating those few tender words she
turned and her dark gaze came up to study his
grim, hard visage. 'Yes,' she said, with an insight
that startled him. 'You know all about grief, don't
you, Mat?'

He compressed his thin lips and studied the
scuffed boot on his left foot before looking up and
meeting her steady gaze. He nodded. 'Some.'

'Wade said he thought you should attend the
funeral,' she said. 'After all, you gunned down
father's killer.'

Immediately, Fallon's warning senses became
animal-keen. He became sharply alert, his brain
probing for reasons why Wade Coleman, of all
people, would want him to attend the burial of
Wyatt Marsden.

'That doesn't sound like the Coleman I knew,' he rasped harshly, hardly able to contain his loathing for the man.

Jane looked surprised by his sharp reply. 'You know Wade?'

Fallon nodded bleakly. 'Some.'

Again he felt compelled to pour out all the knowledge he had of Wade Coleman, but he bit it back. At the moment, Jane was hurt enough. Even though withholding his knowledge stuck in his craw.

Jane was saying, 'So will you?'

Fallon nodded and said, 'Proud to, Jane.'

And, for the first time, she smiled. 'Twelve o'clock.'

Fallon returned the smile, his hard face altering pleasantly as he did. 'Fine with me, ma'am.'

He watched her as she returned to the house.

Serious thoughts buzzed around in his mind now. Wade Coleman wanted him at the burial. It was more in character for Coleman to want him dead, as he had threatened in no uncertain terms.

Fallon narrowed his grey, flinty eyes. This burial should prove to be interesting.

*   *   *

Folks began arriving at the Lazy M until the bare ground before the big ranchhouse was full with horses, buckboards, gigs, and surreys. Soon folks were walking around with drinks and food in their hands, picked up from the laden trestle tables set out before the ranchhouse for just such a purpose, and talk was low and respectful.

Fallon had watched Coleman arrive about ten o'clock, soon after Jane had talked with him. Jane met the saloon owner at the ranchhouse door. Coleman had swept off his black homburg, taken her arm, and escorted her inside.

Seeing it, Fallon's sombre eyes turned to hard flint. He stared at the dull sky. Clouds brooded over the big range and he felt sweaty in the humid air. If only he could show Coleman in his true colours, his thoughts niggled. He spat fiercely into the dust and growled with frustration.

By twelve o'clock the people had migrated to the graveside and the preacher from Greenville was conducting the sad funeral service, adding a moving postscript about Wyatt Marsden, the man.

With other range hands, Fallon had placed himself a little apart, at the rear of the hundred-strong congregation. Two waddies he recognised as being High Baldy riders, members of the card school at the stage post at Tonto Springs.

Fallon felt on edge, nervous, and could not get the uneasy thoughts out of his mind as to why Coleman wanted him at the funeral. Repeatedly, he scanned the range for something, but what? What could there be to look for? Ambush was almost out of the quest –

The boom of a big rifle cut in harshly on his

ruminations, drowning out the voice of the preacher. A sharp gasp came from the waddy beside Fallon as he staggered back, his arm broken and spurting blood.

Immediately, Fallon tensed. He had heard that big sound before. It was the noise Brink Mather's Sharps had made that day back in the hills when he had shot at him.

He ducked down, ignoring the harsh pain that stabbed from the still sore wound in his side. All around, men and women were doing the same, some women screaming. Most of the people gathered had walked up, Fallon knew. He was one of the few who had ridden up.

Now he limped towards the bay, ground-hitched nearby, all the time his gaze searching the range in the direction the shot had come from. And he thanked God that the man who had been on the butt end of that big rifle was not greatly skilled in the art of long-range fire.

His gaze found what he looked for now. Yes, a ball of dust was roiling up from the sombre range, melding into the grey, threatening sky.

With anger, like a burning coal in his gut, Fallon climbed atop his bay. The Mather brothers were turning out to be, as he had always suspected, nothing but deep-down coyotes.

'Git!' he commanded his horse, harshly.

As he headed off down the slope, his fierce glare found Coleman's cold, black look. Coleman looked angry, too, and that gave Fallon some comfort as he headed for the rise of dust.

FOUR

Half an hour later Fallon cut the bushwhackers'
trail. Two riders. It led him into broken, rocky
ground some five miles south of the Lazy M.

By the time he reached the rocks, pain racked
him unmercifully. Gritting his teeth, he jutted his
strong jaw aggressively, steeling his will, angered
by his weakened state.

So torturous was the pain now he had to slow
the bay down to a walk to cope with it. And having
to do so inevitably meant the Mathers would be
long gone! He knew it was just his dogged
stubbornness that was keeping him on their trail.

But, bringing him to full alertness despite his
pain and irritation, came the thunder of hooves
from behind.

Eyes narrow, he hoisted his Colt and edged into
the cover of the rocks. Four riders swung round
the huge boulder he had just negotiated and he
relaxed and pouched his piece when he saw them.
Two he recognised as the High Baldy riders he'd
seen at the funeral.

The party drew rein the moment they saw him.

One hard-eyed rider looked at him doubtfully, but respectfully. 'You look all in, Fallon,' he said. 'We'll take it from here. That was a High Baldy rider's arm that damned bastard near shot off.'

Fallon bit back his pain and nausea. 'That slug was meant for me, boys,' he gritted meaningly. 'I know who they are.'

The riders leaned forward and four pairs of surprised narrow eyes quizzed him.

'How d'you know?' one rider demanded.

'They've tried before with that big rifle,' Fallon informed. 'There ain't many of those cannons around.'

Fallon could feel sweat running freely from him now as the combination of humidity, pain and exhaustion assailed him. 'I figure them to be Brink and Chance Mather, or I'll eat sheep dung,' he said. 'They've been doggin' my trail some time. The 'why' of it I ain't goin' into right now.'

Again, hard rangemen's eyes studied him. 'Well,' another said, 'no matter who they are, Fallon, it's up to us.'

Anger and frustration simmered in Fallon to feel so frail. He wanted like hell to be on the Mather brothers' trail. He'd run from them long enough. He should have ended it long ago. He had hoped the boys would have given up and gone home. Knowing them all these years he'd have bet money Chance would have done. But Brink ...? Not that damned sour-gutted bastard!

'Got to be my business, boys,' he gritted but had to clench strong teeth against the fresh spasms of pain that hit him.

The tall rider who had spoken first, said, 'You're swayin' like an aspen in a high wind, Fallon. You ain't fit for this shindig. And you must understand – when those two cut down our pard, Jim, it became our business, too.'

Fallon nodded, too weak to argue. He felt light-headed. And he found exposing the feebleness he felt, even to friendly men, harrowing and degrading. But he had to admit to himself, no matter how bitter the pill, he was in no shape to meet the Mathers, even if he could catch up with them.

'Well, watch yourselves, boys,' he said. 'They're a mean pair.' He met four pairs of keen eyes looking at him, individually. 'I'd appreciate hearing how you get on,' he added.

The spokesman nodded, hard-faced. 'We owe you that.' Then, as if not wanting to waste more time, the rangeman wheeled his horse and grunted, '*Adios*, Fallon.'

Grim-faced, the other riders turned with him and took off.

Fallon watched until the rangemen lost themselves in the rough ground ahead before reluctantly swinging his bay round and heading back to the Lazy M, his frailty now acute, his anger, because of it, savage.

He reckoned he must have been fifteen minutes down-trail when the crack of the rifle and the hum of lead past his ear sent him scrambling out of the saddle, dragging his Winchester with him and rolling desperately into a depression in the ground nearby, gasping harshly at the pain it caused.

Whistling shrilly the bay turned and hoofed off to stand some distance away, snorting.

His breath rasping in his throat Fallon's now alert, steely gaze found the rise of ground some hundred yards ahead: the only cover there was. Whoever it was that had shot at him had to be behind that, he reasoned.

He stared at the rimline, the adrenalin now pumping through him dulling the nagging soreness in his side and the pervading nausea it engendered, pushing him into a state of high watchfulness.

As he stared, a slow, heavy drizzle started to fall. Feeling it, he spat sourly and cursed, knowing he had no slicker with him.

But distracting him from that natural disgust, movement came from up ahead – the top of a black hat edging along the skyline of the hill.

Fallon watched it, his muscles tightening. But held his fire. If it was the old trick, he wasn't falling for it, he decided. He only dealt lead when he had something real to hit.

The hat disappeared.

Fallon's whole body tensed now. He blinked once as he sent his hard gaze scanning the length of the rim of the hill. He hardly noticed that, with the drizzle, mist was creeping in.

He was looking right when movement to his left spurred him into a quick, anxious turn, his steely eyes sighting up the Winchester on the small target the man now pointing the rifle at him presented.

This time lead smacked off Fallon's stetson, sending it into the wet grass yards behind him, but his own cluster of three shots blended with the crack of the rifle ahead. And grim pleasure filled him to hear the cry of pain from his assailant as he disappeared with alacrity behind the hill.

Keen and expectant now, Fallon blinked again and rolled twice to alter his position. Now he shook away the sweat and rain dripping from his forehead and stared, taut and watchful – ignoring his hurts – for further movement.

The sound of pounding hooves shattered the tense silence that had descended over the grey range. His ears straining, his eyes steel chips, Fallon heard them go silent behind the swell of ground before him.

Hot talk came now.

Maybe a minute passed, then Jane Marsden rode over the hill at the head of at least a dozen riders. Wade Coleman was mounted on his big chestnut by her side, wincing with pain and holding his bleeding arm.

At the sight of her Fallon cautiously rose from the hollow and lowered his rifle, hard wariness in his eagle stare.

Her dark eyes were round and questioning as she pulled rein before him. She looked bloated in the baggy yellow slicker she had on. The riders behind her wore waterproofs, too.

'Wade said you shot at him without warning,' she accused him immediately, her face clearly mirroring her surprise and puzzlement at the news.

Fallon's eyes were cold and glittering and he stared at Wade Coleman, glad to see the pain on the saloon owner's face and the blood seeping through the fingers clasped to his upper right arm. Then he turned his gaze to Jane, again becoming aware of the fierce pain in his side returning as the adrenalin ceased to flow.

'He's a liar,' he said bleakly. 'It was the other way around.'

Disbelief came to Jane's eyes. Her stare challenged him. 'Why ...? Why would Wade want to kill you, or you, him?'

'I know too much about him,' Fallon declared.

The decision to talk came swiftly to him. It was no longer any use hiding the truth from Jane.

'What is that supposed to mean?' she demanded.

Water ran off her cream stetson as, perplexed, she looked down at him from atop her horse. It splashed wetly on to her slicker.

Fallon met her now arched stare boldly. 'I knew him seven years ago north of here, in a place called Cayton Town. I know he's been to jail for six years for land-grabbing, running a crooked gambling house, and suspected murder – though that wasn't proved. But everybody knowed, even if he hadn't done it, he'd had his paid gunsels to do the killin' that caused the mayhem on the range.'

He watched stark disbelief come to Jane's face

as she listened to his calm, matter-of-fact statement. Her mouth worked for moments, but no words came out. Then she managed to gasp, 'It's got to be lies. Wade's decent, honest.'

Fallon narrowed his stare, resenting the implication that he was a liar, even though it was obvious Jane had been knocked sideways by his revelations.

'Jane,' he growled, 'you asked me; I'm tellin' you.' He blinked now as the drizzle turned to heavy rain and began to patter down on to the range. He went on, 'Not only that, I figure he had my Pa gunned down, too. And when I faced him over it in that gamblin' den he had, he had me near shot to death from behind.'

Fallon, anxious now to be believed, carried on, 'And another thing, ma'am, the man who murdered your father – Harn Faber – was Coleman's paid assassin during that time.'

Jane made a moaning, hurt noise and her hand trembled to her mouth, as if she found the words incredible. She turned to Coleman, her dark eyes pleading. 'Wade ... tell me it's lies.'

Fallon's flinty look turned and met Coleman's evil stare. Drenched, the saloon keeper sat his horse, his black mourning suit and homburg sagging under the deluge of rain. But he appeared not to notice it as he turned to Jane who was looking appealingly at him.

'Honey,' he said, voice smooth and firm, 'it wasn't, and isn't, like it sounds.' He nodded his still-handsome head briskly now, ignoring the water spraying off his hat, as if he was impatient to tell his version of the story – get it out of the way. 'Yes, I went to jail for six years,' he admitted. 'I got a year's remission for good behaviour. And yes, I ran a gambling house in Cayton Town. But, this is how it really was ...'

Coleman paused, as if searching for the right words, and loathing filled Fallon. The saloon owner looked deceptively open and sincere as he raised his voice to be heard above the beat of the rain.

'As you know, honey,' he said, 'I'm a businessman, first and foremost, and when gold was found in the hills above Cayton Town, I took advantage of the situation. And I ask you to believe me when I say I ran as straight a house then, as I do now. It was when the mines petered out and gold got scarce that the miners turned nasty. They began to throw all sorts of accusations around; said I ran crooked tables, conned them out of their gold. But the plain truth was – they were just bad gamblers, and bad losers.'

Fallon could see Jane was clearly disturbed by the disclosures suddenly thrust upon her. 'But the land-grabbing,' she ventured, her voice full of anxiety. '*Were* you in it, Wade? And the killer ... this Harn Faber. What about him?'

Fallon watched Coleman nod gravely. The saloon owner's reply came back oozing with sincerity and candour. 'Yes, land-grabbing was going on and men were killing, and being killed, because of it. But, as God's my judge, I had nothing to do with it. When the gold bonanza finished, and the money played out, everybody was looking for a scapegoat, somebody to blame for all the devilry and the mayhem finding the gold had brought upon the town and the range around it.' Coleman paused, his face now heavy and grave. 'Well,' he sighed as though a great injustice had been done to him, 'I was the outsider ...'

With cold anger, Fallon listened to the lies flowing from Coleman. Unable to hold his ragged disgust any longer he stepped forward. 'Why, you damned lyin' cheap-skate,' he breathed.

Jane cut the air with her hand and angrily turned her dark eyes to meet Fallon's hard stare. 'Wait! Let Wade finish.'

Fallon growled, red fury in him, but held his peace out of respect for Jane. He stood glaring at Coleman, dark menace in his eyes. He was hardly able to contain himself as a cold smile, hidden from Jane, crossed the saloon owner's face before turning back to her and going on.

'Well,' he said, 'they decided the scapegoat had to be me. As for Harn Faber ...' Coleman's look was candid when it met Jane's. 'Sure, I hired him to protect me, and I make no apology for it. Those were dangerous days. Miners are hard, tough men, as are cowhands.'

Fallon now became aware that Coleman's eyes were turning on to him again, this time taking Jane's stare with his. Then the saloon owner said harshly, his finger pointing and accusing, 'Why, out of his own mouth, Jane, Fallon has admitted to you he came into my establishment in Cayton Town to shoot me down, believing I had something to do with his father's killing.'

At that, rage blazed through Fallon. 'You did,' he grated, 'you low-down lyin' skunk!'

Jane, as if galvanised by his outburst, turned blazing eyes on to him. 'Let Wade finish!' she said again.

Gloating, Coleman hunched forward in the saddle. 'Well, I knew *nothing* about his father's killing,' he said, 'and said so at the time.'

His stare was icy now as it left Jane to challenge Fallon. 'But he wouldn't listen,' he went on, swinging his gaze back to Jane. 'He was out for a killing and had me in his sights. Well, I tell you, had I not had Faber there then, to protect me, I wouldn't be here now, defending myself.' Coleman carried on, arrogantly, 'I guess he still figures, in some bull-headed way, it was me that had his father shot, and it's stuck in his craw all these years. I reckon that's why he tried to bushwhack me now!'

Dramatically, Coleman pointed an accusing finger. 'If anybody is a murderer here, Jane, it's Fallon. He doesn't tell you he did two years for robbery with violence, does he?'

Fallon, his wrath now ripe to hear such distortions of the truth, stepped forward, dropped his rifle and clawed his hand above his Colt. 'God damn you, you mangy, gut-low coyote, slap leather!' he rasped harshly, his anger nearly choking him.

Guns slid out from under wet slickers. 'Don't even think about it, Fallon,' came a rangeman's hard warning. 'Coleman don't carry sidearms.'

Frustrated now, Fallon swung his gaze. He could see no bulge under Coleman's riding-coat.

Obviously triumphant, Coleman blinked, happy the riders were siding with him. He turned, ignoring Fallon's raging stare, and looked disarmingly at Jane.

'Honey, as God's my judge, I didn't know it was Harn Faber who gunned down Wyatt. I haven't seen him for over seven years. To me, he was a gunfighter hired to protect me, at a time I needed protecting. That was all. Whoever hired him to kill Wyatt, it wasn't me.' Coleman looked hurt now, his dark eyes appealing to Jane's stricken gaze. 'Jane, I came here to create a new life for myself. I have built up a sound business and have met the sweetest gal in the county. Now, I ask you, why would I, of all people, want to have your father gunned down?'

Clearly moved Jane swung round on Fallon, her eyes, though tear-filled, hot and angry. 'Well, what is your answer, Mat?'

Seething with frustration, Fallon held her stare. Coleman's performance had been outstanding. He knew he had been torn apart by an expert.

'He's lying, Jane,' he said then. He endeavoured to put hard warning into his voice. 'He's very good at it. It saved him from the gallows at Cayton Town.'

Jane arched her neck, her face haughty and

disbelieving, and clearly distressed by the revelations.

'Is that the best you can do?' she challenged. 'And why should I believe you?' she insisted. 'I've known Wade two years and found him an honourable, truthful man. I've known you three days.'

Now she demanded, her face turning hard and hostile, 'Tell me – *have you been to jail?*'

Fallon found a certain desperation building up in him. This wasn't going right at all.

'Like Coleman said, Jane,' he admitted, 'I did two years for robbery – but no violence.' He met her angry stare candidly. 'I was young. Pa got killed and I went off the rails a little, I guess.' He turned cold eyes on Coleman. 'But I know for sure that coyote, choose what he says, had my father killed. And because of it, Ma threw a rope over a beam in the barn and hung herself because she couldn't live without him.'

He met Jane's now appalled stare. She was still clearly agitated. 'Is that why you went after Wade now, because you still think he was behind your father's shooting and your mother's death?' she demanded.

Fallon's gaze was grey, level and cool as he met her dark stare. 'I didn't shoot at him, Jane. He shot at me. An' I'll tell you more: the ambush at the funeral just now ... I believe the men involved in it to be Brink and Chance Mather, men who were part of Coleman's gang during the Cayton Town days.'

Jane gasped, now clearly bewildered by the revelations coming to her. She looked a sad, shattered, forlorn figure in the dreary, rain-soaked afternoon. She turned in the saddle.

'Wade,' she pleaded. 'What is he saying?'

Fallon stiffened, the fires of loathing in him for Coleman as the saloon owner looked as bewildered as Jane with what he had said.

'Honey, what can I say?' he pleaded now. 'I didn't kill his father, or cause his mother to hang herself. I was as appalled as anybody when I heard of it.'

Coleman paused now, his black eyes candid. 'And about Brink and Chance Mather ... Yes, they *are* on this range. I bumped into them the other day. In fact, I took them back to the High Stake and had a drink with them, just for old times' sake. But to say they were part of any gang I was supposed to have had is ludicrous. They had a small ranch on the Cayton range. Occasionally we did a little business.'

Coleman paused and nodded, as if astonished by the things now coming to mind. He looked at Jane earnestly.

'I explained to them I found it odd after seven years of seeing nobody from the Cayton Town days, to see Brink, Chance *and Fallon* – who I explained I had just left at the Lazy M – all on the same day.'

Fallon felt himself filling with a cold anger as the words rolled silkily off the saloon-owner's tongue.

'They told me they were on Fallon's trail,' Coleman was saying, 'because he had killed their father and their brother, James.' As if indignant now that he should be here arguing his case at all, Coleman's voice was rasping.

'Why, don't you see, Jane?' he demanded *'Fallon is a killer*. He just tried to kill me again. He thought I was alone, because, in my eagerness to track down the ambushers, I'd got a head-start on you. He has killed James Mather and the old man – and Harn Faber, albeit, in your defence and your father's. But a killer, Jane. *A killer.'*

Fallon met Jane's now horrified look as she turned to him, giving the impression she didn't want to believe it.

'Have you killed these men?' she said, her voice hardly above a whisper.

Fallon compressed his grim lips. Damn it, this wasn't the way it was at all. Couldn't she see Coleman was lying? He blinked steely eyes, ignoring the rain pattering down on the sombre gathering.

'James Mather called me out,' he informed bleakly. 'Well ... he lost and the rest of the Mather clan figured I should pay for it and lit out after me. They stopped me on the trail. Though outnumbered three to one, the outcome was, I shot old man Mather dead, winged Brink and escaped. Now, it seems, they figure to bushwhack me.'

Jane's eyes dulled. Fallon was surprised to see she looked sad, even a little disappointed.

'You are a gunfighter,' she breathed.

Fallon shook his head, his face set and grim.

'No, ma'am,' he said firmly. 'I was a farmer, now I'm a survivor. I ain't goin' to allow any man to ride me into the ground without he has to fight like the devil to do it.'

Clearly, Fallon could see indecision plagued Jane. She looked unhappily from Coleman to himself.

Then she said, quietly, lowering her gaze, her voice hardly audible above the drum of the rain. 'Mat, I have to believe Wade. You see, I agreed to become engaged to him just before the funeral, though it hasn't been announced yet.'

FIVE

Fallon stared, shocked by what he heard and his words just tumbled out of him.

'Don't do it, Jane,' he warned harshly. 'Coleman's a devil. He ain't fit to lick your shoes.'

Coleman, as if galvanised by the cutting words, leaned forward aggressively in the saddle, his wound apparently forgotten.

'Damn it,' he hissed. 'I don't have to take this.'

Fallon turned to him, ignoring the guns and hard stares that were on him.

'Then, what are you goin' to do about it, Coleman?' he grated. 'You've got a rifle …'

Evil dwelled in Coleman's stare for moments, before he masked it and nodded.

'Yes,' he breathed, 'it would be easy for you, wouldn't it, if you tempted me into a gunfight? You know I know little or nothing about guns. To challenge you would be to invite certain death.' He turned to Jane, triumph in his look. 'See how he reacts,' he appealed, 'when truth and reason have defeated him.'

Jane's eyes, Fallon found – when she turned to

look at him – were sad, but not condemning. 'You can stay at the Lazy M until you are healed up, Mat,' she said. 'But, as soon as you are ... I guess, for all our sakes, it would be better if you left.'

Hearing the words, which were hardly audible at the end, Fallon tightened his lips grimly and nodded, grateful at least for her compassion and for not entirely disbelieving him. But ...

'Jane, I'm a target,' he said now, a softness taking the usual hard edge off his voice. 'That much the Mather brothers have made plain. I'll pick up my possibles and leave you in peace.'

'But your wound!' she protested. He met her sudden, appealing look, which seemed to say in some perverse way she wanted him to stay, for a short time at least. 'I owe you for saving my life, Mat. And I won't be intimidated by the possibility of being exposed to violence. We already know, rustlers are riding this range.'

Fallon narrowed his eyelids. 'Yeah, the rustlin',' he grunted. 'I'm coming to the opinion you won't have to look far to find the man behind it.' He stared straight at Coleman, his look as dark as the sky overhead, ignoring the rain pattering down between them.

The saloon owner tensed visibly. His stare was evil when it found Fallon's mocking, challenging eyes. Coleman seemed to be fighting against almost overwhelmingly dark passions writhing within him.

'You won't draw me, Fallon,' he grated. 'Jane has had enough grief for one week. But continue and, by God – '

Fallon was unmoved by the threat in Coleman's harsh words. 'Harn Faber's dead, Coleman,' he barked harshly. 'You ain't got that backshooter to do your killin' now.'

Coleman stiffened, and his body quivered with pent-up anger. His normally tanned features were pale as he turned to Jane.

'Honey,' he said. 'I'll leave. It's clear Fallon's hell bent on provoking me, completely ignoring your feelings and your grief.'

The thunder of hooves coming from the east and the shapes of riders looming out of the rain and mist took the tension out of the situation as all men and Jane turned to the horsemen.

At their head was a tall, very thin, wiry man. His features were hollow and gaunt but his stare was clear-eyed and piercing-blue, looking out from determined, severe features.

'Mace!' Jane Marsden's voice was surprised. 'I expected to see you at the funeral … Something wrong?'

The tall man hunched forward in the saddle, water draining off his greasy brown stetson, his keen eyes surveying her.

'Jane,' the man began, 'I wanted like hell to pay my last respects to Wyatt, and sent what men I could spare to represent me; but the facts are we've been hit agin by these damned rustlers. That makes more than three hundred head I've lost in two weeks. We followed them to the brakes down by the river and on, but the trail was too cold to have any hope of catching them. I guess they're clear over the border by now ...'

Frustration was etched into every line of Mace Readon's leathery face. 'Damn it,' he snorted, 'the High Baldy can't go on takin' these sort of losses, Jane. I lost enough to last winter's snows.'

Fallon studied the rangy High Baldy boss. A man who stood no nonsense was his immediate assessment, but also a man verging on desperation.

Jane was clearly concerned and a frown of puzzlement puckered her brow. 'Why just the High Baldy, Mace?' she speculated. 'As far as I know, the Lazy M hasn't lost a single steer.'

Mace Readon was obviously as baffled as Jane, emphasised by a swift, angry growl. 'I was just about to point that out,' he snorted.

'Have you spoken to Sheriff Milton?' Jane probed now.

Readon nodded, his face bleak and wet with rain. 'Says he knows of no other rustlin' in the county. But he's gettin' on to it. Says he already has suspicions.' Readon spat. 'But damn it, Jane, I want answers, not suspicions.'

Readon looked round now at the group of Lazy M riders and at Wade Coleman, but Fallon found the longest stare was allotted to him – and the guns pointed at him.

'Who's this?' Readon asked, his gaze steely and suspicious as it stared through the rain and mist.

Jane stirred in the saddle, her slicker crackling dryly. 'Mat Fallon. He's the man who saved my life and shot down father's killer.'

Readon's blue stare widened, then narrowed. Fallon met the rancher's probing gaze with steady grey eyes as it turned to find him. He read a certain respect in it.

'So you're Fallon,' Readon said. 'What business brings you on this range, mister ... and why the guns on you?'

Fallon met the rancher's keen, intrigued look with steady grey eyes. 'I was passin' through,' he offered. 'In answer to your other bit – I said a few things that weren't liked.'

Readon's gaze probed more before he said, 'You a gunfighter?' The question was brisk and abrupt.

Fallon shook his head fiercely, not wanting that kind of tag placed on him, resentment rising in him at the suggestion. Yet, on the face of it, it was a reasonable enough assumption, he thought grudgingly.

'I've been working cows for the last four years,' he countered.

Readon persisted. 'You haven't answered my question.'

Fallon was finding being wet through and sore with pain and suspected of being a gunman was making him ever more irritable.

'You've got all I'm prepared to give,' he said crisply.

He turned, ignoring the guns on him and caught his bay and swung up into the saddle and pouched his rifle.

As he pulled his horse round to face the riders,

Readon said, 'There's a job on my payroll for a man like you.'

Fallon stared at the rancher, not attempting to hide his surprise.

'Why? Because I can use a gun?' Fallon held Readon's bright blue gaze. 'For all you know I could be neck-high in this rustlin'.'

Fallon thought he saw the suggestion of a smile in Readon's eyes. 'I go a piece on gut-feelin's, Fallon,' the rancher said. 'I've got a feelin' about you.'

Fallon calmed. It was nice, for once, to be trusted. He felt he owed Readon a warning.

'I'm in all kinds of trouble at the moment, Mr Readon,' he said. 'You'd be better without me.'

Readon's eyes narrowed. 'What trouble? To do with the guns on you?'

Looking at the rancher Fallon had a feeling that, although it had appeared a spontaneous decision on Readon's part to employ him, and he had confessed it was a gut-feeling, it had actually been swiftly and thoroughly thought out while the talk had gone on.

He said, 'Maybe you should ask Miss Jane. She's offered me a bunk until I'm healed up, though I don't figure on takin' it.'

Readon turned and looked at Jane now with narrowed eyelids. 'What does he mean?'

Jane, responding to Readon's abrupt question, told of the bushwhacking attempt at the Lazy M, and the High Baldy hand who stopped the bullet. And also of Fallon's bull-headed – as she saw it –

refusal to expose her to more ambushers' bullets. But nothing about his knowledge and suspicions concerning Wade Coleman.

Readon's gaze was keen and full of questions as it rested on Fallon again. Mat met his gaze calmly.

Readon said, 'These bushwhackers ... you know them?'

Fallon nodded.

Readon pressed him. 'Could there be a tie-in with the rustlers?'

'They've been known to dabble,' Fallon informed.

Readon's gaunt face lengthened, his narrow eyes questioning.

'The hell you say.' His head craned forward now, his eyes bright. Then he said, surprising Fallon with his insight,

'I figure you ain't finished here, Fallon. I figure you won't rest until those gunsels doggin' you are where they belong.' He looked round and his eyes rested on Wade Coleman and stopped there for moments before swinging back to Fallon. 'I figure there's something else that ain't finished here, too. Am I right?'

Fallon narrowed his eyes, disturbed by Readon's perception. He felt he could work for this man with no qualms if he were allowed to operate with a relatively free hand.

'About that job, Mr Readon,' he said, pointedly avoiding saying anything about Coleman to save Jane further embarrassment. 'At the moment I'm shot up. Figure I may have to move easy for a few days.'

Readon's eyes narrowed. 'How many days?'

Fallon pursed his lips. 'Hard to tell. Depends what comes up, I guess.'

Again Fallon found the rancher's startling blue eyes studying him. 'I figure you hard enough to move right now if the need to do so was strong enough,' he said.

Fallon was not quite prepared to accept that assessment of his character, though, again, if the Mather brothers showed up right now, he'd follow them to hell and gone and be damned how weak he felt. He felt sick to his stomach now at having given up so easily when he had first ridden out after them.

He blinked rain out of his eyes. 'You do, eh, Mr Readon,' he said. 'What do you pay?'

Satisfaction that he had been right about Fallon seemed to settle in Readon's look. 'We can discuss that on the ride to the High Baldy.'

'I git a free hand when I need it?' Fallon pursued.

'Don't see why not,' Readon agreed. 'I want these rustlin' sonsofbitches dead, or off my range.'

Fallon turned to meet Jane Marsden's stare, her eyes dark pools as they met his gaze. He had the feeling that he had sown some seeds of uncertainty regarding Coleman.

'I figure it will be better this way, Jane,' he said.

'You are free to do as you like, Mat,' she returned. Fallon found himself not quite convinced that Jane was all that eager to see him go, nor was he all that pleased to be going. 'Perhaps, after what has been said, it would be better, as I explained.'

Fallon turned back to Readon now. 'As Jane said, four of your riders are already after the bushwhackers. It would be a pity if they killed them. Maybe the Mather brothers could tell us somethin'.'

Readon sighed and shook off the moisture beading his sideburns. 'We'll have to wait for the boys to get back to nail that one,' he growled.

SIX

The rain petered out an hour before sunset leaving a darkened, dank, mist-shrouded range.

Mace Readon was hunched in the saddle, his long face serious and full of hollows in the pale light.

Fallon sat erect on his bay beside him, gritting his teeth against the pain throbbing in his side.

He had picked up what possibles he had in the Lazy M bunkhouse and, in the company of the High Baldy riders, had pressed on to Readon's ranchhouse.

The pay Readon had offered was more than satisfactory. Now, as they entered the hilly country north-east Readon said,

'Right, Mat, I'd appreciate the full story. The Lazy M had guns on you. Must have been some good reason.'

Fallon looked long and hard at the High Baldy boss before speaking. Readon seemed a straight, no-nonsense, honest man. And a man not to suffer fools lightly.

Fallon told it truthfully and fully. All that Jane

had left out concerning Wade Coleman. As he unfolded the story, from the death of his father and mother to the events this afternoon, and the suspicions that went with it, Readon was nodding and grunting as if the things he was saying were being confirmed in the rancher's own mind. When Fallon finished he found Readon's blue, eager stare upon him.

'I knew it,' he said. 'That low-down sonofabitch. Wyatt Marsden had no time for him, neither do I. Wyatt was as sore as a tick-troubled longhorn bull when Jane took a shine to him. Wyatt wouldn't have seen her wed to him at any price.'

Fallon said, his eyes narrowing, interested to hear the opinion, 'Didn't he take steps to stop it?'

Readon nodded his head fiercely. 'Sure he did. All he could. But Jane's a wilful young lady, and, I guess, old enough to know her own mind. But sometimes females act stupid when they take a real shine to a man. They can't see beyond their noses. And that was the way it was, and is, I guess. Wyatt just had to tolerate Coleman callin', hoping somethin' would happen to change Jane's mind. He loved Jane too much to throw her out for disobeying him.'

Not too surprised with the information and Readon's reaction to Coleman, Fallon observed they had now entered a wide valley at the head of which was an upthrust of grey, dome-headed limestone rock. That had to be what gave High Baldy its name, he reasoned. Sure enough, Fallon saw, as they topped a rise, a long, low ranchhouse nestled some half-mile away from the foot of it, plus the usual outbuildings.

He said now to Readon, 'Have you any ideas where the rustlers may be holed up?'

Readon pulled at his long, lean, square jaw. 'Got to be in these hills,' he reasoned. 'It's the only real cover there is on the range.'

Fallon probed, 'You seen any new faces recently?'

'Nothin' permanent,' Readon supplied with a worried sigh. 'Just riders passin' through. Sheriff Cap Milton says there's been some movement of new faces in and out of town, but nothing specific. And no faces he can put wanted notices to.'

The sharp crackle of rifle fire off in the trees up the hillside west of them had Fallon and the group of High Baldy punchers riding hard to the cover of a copse of aspens that stood by a stream two hundred yards to their right. Amongst the trees, all dismounted and took Winchesters to hand.

'What the hell ...?' demanded Readon irately when they were settled in cover. His blue, questioning stare met Fallon's steel-grey look.

Fallon shook his head and scanned the hillside, made drab by the day's torrential rain and now the thin mist. A volley of shots came this time, rattling through the branches above them. He calculated it was maybe six hundred yards to the trees up there.

At that range, Fallon studied, there seemed little point in the bushwhackers shooting, except to send the High Baldy riders running for cover.

And it posed the question, had they disturbed something …?

Fallon found he wanted to know more.

He blinked as he looked at Readon. 'You reckon you could cover me while I take half a dozen hands and try to get round behind them? I reckon we've stumbled on to somethin'.'

Readon's stare was questioning. 'Like what?'

Fallon set his chin. 'Rustlin'?'

Readon looked incredulous at the suggestion. 'This close to the ranch?'

'Why not?' Fallon pointed out, 'We've passed some mighty sleek beeves on the way in. And with you on the trail of the last passel that was lifted, other High Baldy men at Marsden's funeral …' Fallon stare was probing now. 'How many men have you got at the ranchhouse?'

It was obvious from Readon's look that there was hardly a man left manning the place.

As if to confirm Fallon's suspicions, Readon brought a gnarled fist down on to the bole of the tree he was taking cover behind.

'Damn them,' he snarled. 'And damn their gall!' His face altered to one of questioning as he looked to Fallon's wounded side before returning his gaze.

'You figure you're up to it?' Readon's look was doubtful.

'I'm offerin', ain't I?' Fallon returned.

For some time now he'd realised his whole being had been railing against the gnawing pain from his wound. He'd hardly been able to hold his anger at having to suffer it and be incapacitated by it. Damned if he'd let it beat him any longer, he'd decided finally; or the tiredness the loss of blood had caused.

'What good do you think it'll do?' Readon was saying.

'Set them wonderin' an' worryin', and maybe get us a herd of beeves back,' Fallon said. 'If we head out towards the ranchhouse before we double back ...' Fallon hardened his stare. 'I have a gut-feelin' things are movin' behind that ridge yonder, and not in your interest ...'

As he voiced his opinions, riders burst out from the trees further to the north of the valley. And one was obviously hurt. They were heading straight for the High Baldy ranchhouse.

Fallon felt sure he recognised two of the riders. He studied Readon's gaunt features. 'Looks like the men that went after the Mather brothers,' he opined seriously.

Readon's look was bleak. 'Yeah ... They're High Baldy, sure enough.'

Sudden anger blazed in the rancher's eyes. 'Damn it, now they're shootin' my hands.' Fallon met his incensed stare. 'Well, I ain't standin' for that,' the rancher growled. 'We're goin' to rush those sonsofbitches.'

Fallon felt his gut tighten.

'With respect, Mr Readon,' he ventured, 'that'd be a dumb play. They'd mow us down like wheat. No, I figure they're coverin' somethin'; pinnin' us down while they get on with some other business ...'

The rancher's keen eyes narrowed, his stare searching. 'You ain't backin' away, are you, Fallon?'

Fallon tightened inside, but decided Readon was entitled to be suspicious. To the rancher, he was a total stranger. He felt it was time to give some reassurance.

'Ain't in my make-up, Mr Readon,' he said firmly. 'But I can be a cautious man.'

Fallon watched Readon's eyes narrow as he spoke and he found the rancher's hard stare studying him as if looking for some weakness or flaw in his make-up he hadn't spotted before. And it was obvious he wasn't used to having his directives questioned.

But Fallon had assumed the rancher was prone to impetuousness when he had abruptly offered him a job, hardly knowing a thing about him. But if he was prompted to reconsider with sound argument ...

He waited and watched as Readon studied the lie of the land between the trees for seconds before grunting,

'OK ... what business?'

Fallon could see Readon was not entirely pleased with his caution.

But satisfaction settled in Fallon to have Readon listen. 'I want to see what's behind that ridge,' he said. 'My guess is they have a herd assembled there.'

The riders heading for the ranchhouse now

veered towards them, their horses extended belly-low to the range.

The rifle fire from the trees rose, but the range was too great to be either accurate or effective. It convinced Fallon completely now that they were just being pinned down while a herd was being moved.

Readon looked at the sullen sky and rubbed his chin, his look thoughtful. 'It'll be dark soon,' he opined. 'They'll cut and run under cover of darkness, maybe.'

He turned to his men pressed against tree-boles, rifles lined up on the trees up the hillside. He briskly called six names. 'Ride out with Fallon,' he ordered. 'Do as he says.' He turned and Fallon – who, when he had heard the command, was already climbing into the saddle – met his stare. 'See what those sonsofbitches are up to,' he said.

Fallon grinned, but his face was tight and pale. 'Will do, Mr Readon.' He looked at the men beginning to climb into saddles. When they were settled he said, 'Let's go, boys.'

Fallon felt satisfaction wash through him as he topped the ridge crest. Sure enough, in the narrow valley below, riders were hazing a fair-sized herd of beeves. He counted seven men.

He looked at the range around him now, darkening quickly, then at the six grim-faced rangemen staring at him intently.

'We've got to relieve them of that herd, boys, before it's dark,' he said. 'So let's go!'

He put the bay into a gallop and was within rifle range before the rustlers realised they were being attacked. Fallon squeezed off three times, but found targets elusive, hard to hit from the back of a running horse. But, satisfaction in him, saw the scare-factor was working.

High-pitched, alarmed whoops came from the riders below. They began immediately to scatter, the herd forgotten.

Fallon felt further satisfaction as his fifth shot found a target. The owlhoot swayed, before clinging desperately to the saddle of his running piebald.

Gunfire was hotting up now. Angry snapping reports echoing into the hills. Because of it, the herd was beginning to run, scattering into the trees and along the grassy base of the narrow valley they were in.

Fallon was pleased to see it was just a scatter and not a full-blooded stampede.

He turned his attention back to the owlhoots. They were drawing into a bunch now and heading north-west.

Fallon found the bay underneath him was not as lively as he would have liked. But he knew she had been hard pressed this day and therefore must be tired.

Acknowledging in his mind that they might be unable to run the rustlers down he sought another target. Missed. Then he became aware of lead hissing past him and ricochets snarling off the trees to his right and rifle reports coming from above him.

A nearby puncher gave a harsh cry and dropped out of the saddle to roll several times before becoming still.

Fallon swung his stare up to the ridge line above them. He had half expected it. They must be the owlhoots that had had them pinned down in the next valley. They must have deduced what was happening, Fallon decided, when he had led his men over the ridge and felt the herd more important than holding down Readon and his men.

Realising assistance had come, the rustlers with the herd drew rein and swung round their mounts. Grim urgency came to Fallon.

They were, in essence, surrounded!

The High Baldy riders had realised the situation as well. Fallon found them pulling their mounts to a walk and looking at him for instructions.

Fallon brought his horse to a standstill and looked around him. There was only one thing for it and that was to take to the shelter of the stand of pines nearby and wait for Readon to come over the ridge top.

He pointed to it. 'In there, men!'

They didn't need further prompting.

Fallon found the trees close packed and he had difficulty getting the bay to squeeze into cover. But that could work well for them. It meant the only way in for the owlhoots was on foot, too.

He settled behind a tree-bole and picked his

first target. This time he did not miss and had the satisfaction of seeing his target catapult back and crash into the grass, not to move again.

The withering fire from the rangehands brought the owlhoots up smartly and sent them scattering to reform in the gloom some five hundred yards away. Misty dark was settling fast on the wet range.

Fallon could see now a lively debate was going on amongst the owlhoots. With narrow eyes he studied them. From what he could discern in the gloom, they were hardcases to a man.

Suddenly, scything into his ruminations came the savage rip of gunfire from the ridge above. Fallon realised, with satisfaction, it had to be Readon and his men and relieved whoops came from the men with him in the trees.

Obviously alarmed the owlhoots turned to view the ridge. They must have a better view than himself, Fallon decided, being closer. Himself, he could only see darkness, except for the orange-yellow flashes of gunfire.

Bunching up, the rustlers put their mounts into a gallop toward the hills north-west to be swallowed up by the gloom rapidly intensifying into a soup-dense blackness. Elated, Fallon and his men followed them with shouts and lively fire.

The hard drum of hooves from the south heralded the approach of Readon and his men. Fallon moved out of the trees to greet them.

Readon dismounted close by and Fallon watched him pace bow-legged towards him.

'Did they have a herd?' the rancher demanded immediately.

Fallon nodded in the dark, his hard face set. 'They've scattered. Shouldn't be hard to gather them.'

Fallon saw respect in Readon's eyes as he found the rancher's blue stare on him.

'You were right, Fallon,' he said. 'You seem to have an instinct for these things.'

Fallon pursed his lips. He didn't seek praise for what was no more than a hunch.

'Worked out fine, I guess,' he said.

Readon shuffled on small, booted feet. 'You reckon they'll be back?'

Fallon shook his head. 'Not tonight. What I saw, they had a couple of men winged and they've left one for dead. We had one man hit, but I think he's okay.'

Readon grunted. 'Well, I guess there's not much we can do now,' he said. 'It's too dark to follow them and the horses are tired. Been on the run most of yesterday and today.'

Fallon agreed. 'Guess that's the size of it.'

He felt weak now the excitement of the past hour was subsiding and the pain in his side was savage.

Readon turned to his men. 'Right, boys, chow time. Pick up the dead owlhoot and bring him with you. We'll go after those owlhoot bastards first thing in the mornin'.'

Fallon coughed and started to build a smoke from his Bull Durham sack. 'I don't want to horn in, Mr Readon,' he began, 'but I reckon not much'll be served by that unless you've got an expert tracker in your crew.'

Readon squinted through the gloom at Fallon who was now lighting his quirley, the yellow light of the match carving hollows in his face.

'We ain't,' the rancher stated flatly.

Fallon drew smoke into his lungs and exhaled, feeling comforted. 'Allow me to poke around a bit, Mr Readon. See what I can stir up.'

Readon studied the tall man before him with narrow eyes. There was a calm, iron-hard quality about him that forced a man to take his ideas seriously.

'If you think it will help,' he said.

Fallon nodded, the end of the quirley fiery-red as he drew another lungful.

'I think it will.'

SEVEN

Breakfast had been eaten noisily at the High Baldy. The bunkhouse buzzed with the events of the past few days. Then riders had left early to gather the beeves scattered yesterday.

The ride to Greenville took Fallon four hours. The trail passed through pretty, low hills and flat monotonous grasslands that went on beyond the town to seeming infinity.

The sun was now high and hot on his back, but the day was fresh and washed clean by the rain.

Fallon hadn't been able to give Readon any coherent plan; he had just said he wanted to poke around, try and lift up a few stones to see what was underneath. He'd decided to start at Greenville and maybe pay the High Stake Saloon a visit.

At that, Readon had narrowed his keen eyes.

'Could prove lively,' he said. 'How's your wound?'

Fallon admitted truthfully, 'It's mending. Feel better.'

'You goin' to prod Coleman into doin' somethin'?' Readon probed now.

Fallon pursed his lips. 'Reckon he's too much savvy to allow that. If I do, it won't be easy.'

There was another thing, too, that had sobered Fallon when he'd heard it. The riders who had gone after the Mather brothers had come under fire from the big Sharps again and this time the fire had been more accurate. The rangeman who had been hit had died during the night.

Fallon found Greenville neat, busy, orderly and prosperous, nestled in the hollow of the range. At the sheriff's office he dismounted.

A deputy was behind the desk, writing. He looked up when Fallon's tall frame darkened the doorway.

'The sheriff about?' Fallon said.

'Eatin' at Fanny Mason's place.'

'He mind his eatin' bein' disturbed?'

The young man screwed up his round, ruddy face thoughtfully. His brown gaze was quizzical.

'Depends what it is, I guess,' he probed.

'Point me in the direction of the eatin' house,' Fallon said. His voice was even, but firm.

'It that important?' the deputy pursued.

'Mace Readon had one of his hands kilt chasin' bushwhackers yesterday,' Fallon provided. 'Also, we ran a passel of rustlers off his land last night.'

The deputy's brown gaze grew hard and sharp as it turned up to meet Fallon's steady stare.

'The hell you say,' he breathed. 'Damn it, they're gettin' to be a nuisance.' After brief moments, his scrutiny still keen, the deputy instructed, 'Turn right out of the door. Fanny Mason's is up the street, on the left – mebbe a hundred yards.'

Fallon's horny finger touched the brim of his grey, greasy stetson.

'Obliged.'

Outside the office his boots rang hollowly on the boardwalk. The people who passed him all eyed him with either curious or suspicious eyes. Fallon looked over them, his eyes searching for the eating-house the deputy had mentioned. He soon found it. A white-painted clapboard structure with Fanny Mason's Eatery blocked above the large front window in red letters. Bluecheck curtains were up at the door and windows.

Inside it was hot and the aroma of meat cooking and vegetables boiling thickened the air, making it moist and clammy.

Fallon looked round the crowded eatery for a sheriff's star. The man wearing it was a tall, tanned, spare man with greying hair and keen, piercing, dark eyes.

He looked up as Fallon approached. He was hacking at a large, rare steak swimming in vegetables and gravy.

Fallon seated himself at the table in the chair opposite the rangy lawman.

'Sheriff Milton?'

Fallon found the stare studying him was narrow and calculating. 'You've found him.'

'Mat Fallon, sheriff –'

'Been hearin' all kinds of things about you, Fallon,' the lawman cut in sharply, his voice brisk.

'Some good, some bad.'

Sheriff Milton shovelled a piece of steak into his wide mouth and chewed hungrily, talking through it. 'Well, state your piece.'

Fallon told of the bushwhacking and the rustling of High Baldy stock and the shooting of the High Baldy riders, also the dead owlhoot.

Between chews Milton said, 'Anybody know the dead rustler?'

Fallon shook his head. 'No, sir. None of the High Baldy hands, or Mace Readon.'

The sheriff drew a piece of gristle from his mouth and laid it on the side of his plate and started hacking at the steak again.

'You workin' for Readon?'

Fallon nodded.

'Why did you shoot at Wade Coleman yesterday?' the sheriff demanded then.

Fallon's only reaction was to blink. 'You've got it a mite wrong, sheriff,' he said. 'He shot at me.'

'Not the way I heard it.'

'You heard it wrong,' Fallon said doggedly.

'You got a beef against Coleman?' Sheriff Milton probed.

Fallon saw no reason to be diplomatic. 'He's a no-account sonofabitch.'

Sheriff Milton's keen, dark gaze now tied with Fallon's hard, uncompromising stare. Fallon felt uneasy. It was as though the lawman was searching his soul. Then, as if he'd made his mind up about him, Milton said abruptly,

'I know of Coleman's background. But he served

his time, paid his dues. And he ain't put a foot wrong in this town.'

Fallon felt unmoved by the statement, but slightly surprised that Sheriff Milton had gone so thoroughly into Coleman's history. He was about to answer when a large woman with round, flushed cheeks came to the table. 'What's your pleasure, mister? You can't sit here without eatin'.'

The sheriff smiled broadly at Fallon. 'Meet Fanny Mason.'

Fallon stared into the eating-house owner's blue, large, enquiring eyes. 'Steak with trimmin's,' he said.

When Fanny Mason had gone he turned back to the sheriff. He decided to be blunt. 'I figure Coleman's behind the rustlin' goin' on on this range.'

Sheriff Milton loaded his large mouth with another filling of meat and veg, seemingly unmoved by the bald statement.

'That's a big accusation. You proof?'

Fallon shook his head. 'No.'

'Then you're wastin' my time, Fallon,' the sheriff said flatly. 'How do I know you ain't in on what you are accusing Coleman of? You're a stranger hereabouts and have served time for robbery.'

Startled, Fallon stared at the eating lawman. It prompted the quick, dry comment from the sheriff: 'Yeah, I know that, too.'

'You do your homework,' Fallon grunted,

thrown by the lawman's thoroughness and directness.

Milton's eyelids narrowed and his look became probing. 'What I know is, you handle guns pretty well and you are on the prod,' he informed. 'What have you got against Coleman?'

'He killed my father, or had him killed by the scum I shot down at Tonto Springs, defending Jane Marsden.' Fallon let his reply ring out harshly. It caused a few eyes to look up from food before dropping again and continuing with the business in hand.

Milton kept on eating, seemingly unimpressed. 'Again … you got proof?' he said through a mouthful of steak.

Fallon growled with frustration and waved an arm. 'It's out there, an' I'll get it,' he promised.

Fanny Mason came with his food. It looked plain but good. He paid what she asked, pleasantly surprised by the reasonable charge. He started to cut at the steak.

Sheriff Milton rose from the table and wiped his mouth on his handkerchief. 'I hope you don't step out of line, Fallon,' he said. There was a brisk warning behind the words. 'Let the law deal with things to do with the law. Do I make myself clear?'

Fallon felt he could promise nothing. 'If I'm shot at, Sheriff,' he said. 'I will shoot back.'

The lawman's dark eyes studied him closely. 'You said you were working for Mace Readon.'

Fallon nodded and chewed on the tasty steak.

'Keep it to cows, mister,' the lawman said

tersely. 'Okay?'

With the narrow-eyed warning Sheriff Milton touched his white stetson and left the steamy eatery.

Fallon's grey gaze followed him. He felt there wasn't a too heavy threat in the lawman's voice, but, whether there was a threat or not, he had a score to settle and a job to do.

Twenty minutes later and feeling satisfied with the meal inside him Fallon breathed deeply as he stood outside the eating house and surveyed Greenville, ignoring the niggling ache in his wounded side.

The streets were quieter, the sun still high and hot. He walked down to the sheriff's office, untied his bay mare and walked it up to the High Stake Saloon and hitched it again.

Inside it was full of drinking men, some eating at tables. He was mildly surprised when Sheriff Cap Milton walked slim and tall towards him from a group of men drinking at the bar.

'I could say this place was out of bounds to you, Fallon,' he attacked immediately, his look stony. 'I don't want trouble in my town.'

'I'm a man who wants a beer, Sheriff,' he countered. 'Is there a law agin that?'

'Heed me, Fallon,' the lawman warned. 'There's a bar up the street.'

Fallon's grey stare was steady, but stubborn. 'There's killin' an' rustling goin' on out there, Sheriff. If you'd allow me I'd like to help.'

Milton was adamant. 'You won't help in here and you know it.'

'To set up the critter, you've got to stir the bushes,' Fallon countered.

'Leave it to me, Fallon,' Milton advised. 'And why are you so damned sure this is the bush?'

Fallon studied the upright, stern man standing before him and the business-like Colt high on his hip. 'Sheriff, I've been shot at twice and near kilt on your range within a week. Now I just can't go on standin' for that.'

Fallon met the lawman's hard stare unflinchingly. 'You ain't an easy man to convince, are you, Fallon?' Milton said then.

The move was so fast it took Fallon completely by surprise. He just wasn't expecting it.

He felt the short barrel of the sheriff's Colt pressing on his stomach, then felt his own gun being eased out of its holster. After looking at the weapon Fallon brought his cold stare up to meet Milton's steady look.

He growled nastily, 'Damn it, what's got into you?'

The lawman's voice was steady. 'I've been tryin' to explain.'

With the producing of the gun the saloon went deathly quiet. Fallon tensed, feeling somehow betrayed. He set his gaze urgently and deliberately searching the saloon and gambling-house for the man he had come to see. Sure enough a door opened at the back of the saloon when the noise dropped. A puzzled Wade Coleman came to the door; beside him was a small, dour-looking man with owlish eyes.

As soon as the saloon owner saw the position he smiled gloatingly, causing Fallon's anger to run warmly through him.

Coleman crossed the floor area quickly, weaving through the tables.

'Well, Sheriff Milton,' he said smoothly, 'it's nice to see the law dealing so efficiently with potential troublemakers.'

Milton's gaze was cold and stern. 'Don't crow over it, Coleman,' he warned harshly.

Now Fallon felt the gun press harder at his stomach.

'Move, mister.'

Fallon strode towards the doorway. The sun was shedding white hot light when he reached the street, still damp from the rain yesterday. His anger seethed inside him. Anger at being caught so easily, and at having the humiliation of being run out of town.

Milton ordered, 'Climb up.'

Fallon eased stiff-legged into the saddle on his bay, never letting his eyes stray from the gun on him. But Milton's stare didn't stop watching him, either, even while the lawman climbed on to the back of his stocky roan.

Milton waved the Colt now. 'Head out the way you came.'

Fallon took up rein and clicked the bay into a walk. Sheriff Milton slotted in behind him, gun level and firm on his back.

All the way out of town, Fallon met the stares that followed him. He was aware eyes still watched their progress as they moved through the edges of the town and beyond.

A mile down-trail Milton said, 'Hold it, Fallon.'

Fallon stopped his bay and turned it and stared at the tall, spare lawman. He was surprised to see the sheriff's gun already back in its workmanlike holster.

'Do I get my gun now?' he said dryly.

Milton unhitched it from where he had stuck it in his gunbelt. He held it then and lifted his gaze to meet Fallon's cold stare.

'I know I ain't popular with you right now, Fallon,' he said. 'But you left me little choice. Whether you were out to start somethin' or not, I wasn't goin' to give you the chance and I tried to make that clear. I won't have trouble in my town. I got votes to think about as well as women an' children. What trouble there's goin' to be I want out on the range.'

Fallon blinked. 'The snake's head is in your precious town, Milton,' he said harshly. 'Cut it off, the rest will die.'

Milton growled. 'You're so damned sure!'

Fallon nodded firmly. 'Yeah.'

He glowered at the sheriff, the force of his conviction obviously disturbing the lawman. Cap Milton seemed to be thinking hard. When he did apparently reach a decision, it was jolting.

'I've had information the owlhoot den is in the hills north,' he said. 'Can you poke around up there for me, Fallon? I'll keep tabs on Coleman. I've a gut-feelin' you're right about him.'

With that the lawman tossed the gun. Fallon caught it and holstered it slowly. He realised he was being asked to work with Milton.

'What then?'

'If you find the den, just report to me.'

Fallon hitched in the saddle, the pressure on his wound uncomfortable. 'I am in the pay of Mace Readon. And I got the Mather brothers doggin' me. Could be I'll have more than I can handle with them.'

Milton nodded. 'Those boys have been in town,' he informed. Again Fallon was taken aback. This lawman was thorough.

'You know them?'

'I have two drawers of wanted notices going back ten years in the office, Fallon,' the lawman said with a proud lift of his head. 'Coleman brought those two sonsofbitches into town, put them up at his boarding house. With his record, it set me riffling through my files.' Milton's eyes were questioning now. 'What you done to them?'

Fallon told it as it happened, from beating James Mather to the draw to the attempted bushwhacking at the Lazy M ranch.

Milton nodded, satisfaction on his lean, tanned features as if something had been confirmed in his mind. 'Well, there's somethin' goin' on,' he admitted. 'An' I'm half-way to knowin' what.'

His gaze lifted and met Fallon's grey stare frankly. 'And I'm with you. I think Coleman is up to his neck in whatever it is. But 'til we have proof, Fallon, it's got to remain a hunch.'

Fallon studied the lawman. Maybe Milton was hogtied by the law, but he wasn't and he felt that was what the lawman was looking for and needing. Somebody who could poke around outside the law.

He blinked. 'I need vittles if I'm goin' to be out in the hills a spell,' he pointed out.

Milton appeared to relax. A grin softened his grim features.

'Lay up here. I'll see you git some.'

EIGHT

To kill time Fallon dismounted and took refuge from the sun under the shade of a cottonwood – part of a cluster beside the trail – and built himself a smoke.

Cap Milton had proved an interesting man, he mused idly. Cautious maybe, but also, he seemed to respond, like himself, to gut-feelings. Fallon raised his brows, struck a sulphur match and lit the quirley.

But he had hardly taken three puffs when the shots from up-trail caused him to sit up – alert, straight-backed and puzzled.

He came to his feet with one lithe movement. He had no doubt the gunfire came from the direction Sheriff Milton had taken.

He narrowed his eyes, his mind working swiftly. Had Milton been shot at, or had the lawman run into some trouble and was dealing with it ...?

Without reasoning any further he caught the bay, stubbed out the quirley and swung aloft. Grimly he put the horse into a run.

He was soon out of the screen of trees hiding the flat range that took the trail into Greenville. Within three minutes he came upon the lawman's horse, standing nervously stomping on the trail. Cap Milton's body lay crumpled and still near it.

Animal-keen senses set Fallon's nerves tingling with wary excitement and he brought his Colt out of its holster. Now his grey, probing stare searched the country around until it found the dust rising from a galloping rider heading for the hills north. Out of habit, Fallon fixed the direction of the man's flight in his mind before dismounting and kneeling beside the moaning sheriff.

'Get a look at him, Sheriff?' he demanded straight-away, while looking at the wound pouring blood from a hole in the middle of the lawman's chest.

Milton's bright, pain-filled stare found his. The lawman shook his head. 'Knew nothin'. Saw nothin'. Jest hit me from cover.'

The sheriff's head rolled now, his eyes hurt and appealing, his teeth bared against the pain. 'God damn it, this ain't right, Fallon,' he protested. 'It ain't supposed to end like th ...'

Stunned, Fallon listened to Milton's last breath sighing out, cutting off his words, rattling through the blood filling the lawman's lungs, mouth and throat.

Fallon looked down at the still face now, the wide-open, staring eyes, hardly believing that Milton was dead, his own senses numbed by the unexpected turn of events.

Suddenly he was alone again. He had felt a certain security and peace of mind when Milton had invited him to work alongside him.

Now ...

The thought was quick and unsavoury when it first came to him: he had to rifle Milton's pockets. Maybe there was something written there, something that could be of use. The lawman had given the impression he knew more than he was prepared to tell him at this phase of their relationship ... and if it would help to nail the lawman's killer and who was behind the rustling ...

He must have knelt there for fully half a minute going through Milton's pockets thoroughly before the click of gun-metal behind him brought him round to stare at the squat, round-faced rider sitting atop his mount, his rifle pointed straight at his midriff.

'You move quiet,' Fallon said, his voice taut.

The man's chin was black with beard stubble, but his grey eyes were cold steel.

'I ought to shoot you down here and now, you scum, on'y that would be too quick,' he growled through yellow teeth. 'You low-down sonofabitch.'

Fallon rose to his feet, staggered by the man's response. The truth came to him swiftly and he gestured disgustedly at the lawman's still body.

'You don't figure I had somethin' to do with this, do you?'

'There ain't anybody else around here as fer as I can see, to say you ain't.'

Fallon felt desperation fill him. 'The man that did this is headin' for the hills right now. I saw his dust.'

A mirthless grin crossed the man's features. 'How come I didn't see it?'

Anger flared through Fallon. 'How the hell should I know? What I do know is, the bastard's puttin' space between me an' him while we yap here.'

The man's face was heavy with scorn. 'Then why weren't you chasin' him instead of robbin' poor Cap there?'

Rage flared through Fallon. 'Damn it, it ain't like that.'

'Ain't it?' The rider growled contemptuously. 'I saw Sheriff Milton escortin' you out of town on the end of his gun not an hour ago,' he said harshly. 'I guess I don't need to look any further than that.'

The rider motioned with his rifle now. 'Un-ship your gun an' drop it, then kneel down, hands behind you,' he demanded. 'You're comin' to town with me.'

Rage filled Fallon's craw. 'Damn it,' he snarled. 'The man who did this is headin' north an' free!'

'Un-ship your piece and git on your knees!' snarled the rider and raised his gun to his shoulder and sighted it menacingly.

Anxiety filled Fallon. For all he knew his own innocence, when this man got him into Greenville and told it as he saw it, there would be only one end as far as he could see – a necktie party with himself as the principal guest, no doubt ably aided and abetted by Coleman.

He moved forward fast, with a reckless audacity born out of desperation, ducking under the rifle and grabbing the man's boot, hooking it out of the stirrup and hefting it upwards, toppling the man.

The rifle cracked once before the rider crashed heavily to the ground on the other side of his chestnut stallion.

Frantically now, Fallon scrambled under the horse's belly on all fours to come up kicking the rifle out of the startled rider's hand. Fallon pulled iron then and stood over the alarmed, sprawling hombre, hammer cocked.

'I told you I didn't do it, mister,' he hissed. 'You should give a man the benefit of the doubt.'

The rider's face turned defiant. 'I caught you clean,' he protested. 'Damn it, I saw you goin' through his pockets –'

'I figured there may have been somethin' to lead me to the killer or the rustlers hereabouts,' cut in Fallon hotly. 'Cap Milton had just asked me to do some scoutin' for him.'

He bent over the man and took his Colt and threw it into the grass.

The rider's face filled with scorn. 'You expect me to believe that? Damn it, he railroaded you out of town!'

Knowing it was useless trying to convince the man of anything, because, admittedly, his actions must have looked bad, Fallon took the rider's lariat off the saddle. He soon had him tied.

'You ain't goin' to leave me here, air you?' The

man's face had gone pale.

Fallon mounted. From atop his horse he stared down at the disbelief on the man's face. 'It looks a well worn trail. I figure you won't have to wait too long for help to arrive.'

'There'll be the biggest posse you ever saw hangin' on your ass when I git free of these, mister,' the rider raged now.

Fallon's look turned steely. 'Think on this, feller, while you're waitin': if I was as black guilty as you think I am you'd be a dead man now. But all you saw was me bendin' over Cap. Use your head, mister, unless your brains are where you sit.'

Without a backward glance Fallon put his mount towards the foothills, intent on picking up the killer's trail.

NINE

Fallon picked up the trail quickly. It led unerringly into the hills. And the deeper he got into them, the more rugged they became, breaking up into tree-clothed ravines and small, verdant valleys.

An army could hide in here, he decided.

Now he found the killer's trail was becoming more difficult. Fading out, causing him to have to quarter the ground to pick it up again. And he paused frequently to study the terrain before him.

It was country built for ambush.

And he felt disappointed that the search through the sheriff's pockets had revealed nothing.

But, whoever had done the shooting – why kill Cap Milton?

Killing the county sheriff was not the most sensible thing to do. And that brought Fallon to the conclusion that Cap Milton had known more than he was telling. And maybe, the person behind the killing of Wyatt Marsden, and the rustling hereabouts – Coleman – guessed the lawman knew more than was good for him – and had dealt with it as ruthlessly as he had dealt with Jane's father.

Fallon's look hardened. But again – why? It just didn't add up. Coleman was too clever for that ...

He now found himself threading his way up a hillside, through thickening trees, culminating in a razor-edged ridge. There was hardly room for his horse to pass. And he also had a prickling feeling, causing the hairs on the nape of his neck to stick up. He was getting near to something. He instinctively knew it. He'd known this feeling more than once and it had been reliable.

He pulled the bay to a stop and listened, while he allowed his gaze to trace the killer's tracks going on up the hillside ahead of him.

Then he heard it. The low of cattle. Admittedly faint, but clear enough not to be mistaken.

Cattle this deep in the hills ...?

He stared ahead, but the firs here were dense enough to cut his field of vision down to twenty yards – thirty yards at the most. But that could be in his favour, he decided. If it cut down his view, it did the same for the owlhoots – if that's who they were, up ahead. And he was growing more confident by the minute that they were.

He edged back down the ridge-side. He felt his hunch very strongly now. There had to be something over the other side of the ridge above him. Every tingling nerve-end in him told him so.

He turned back south again then east, all the time staring up, his eyes searching the higher ground above him.

As he did so, he came to the opinion that, if the owlhoot hideout was over the hill, they had picked it more for its inaccessibility than for the good field of view around it. But, contradicting that, there had to be an easier access, to get the cattle in there.

Some mile or so on he turned east. Here the trees were thinning and the rim of the ridge was losing its sharp, rocky edge.

He gazed up beyond it now to the sky. Behind him the sun was low on the horizon. Another hour and it would be dark.

Then he saw the glint of metal in the rock crevices scarring the ridge top above him.

He drew the bay to a stop, his grim stare seeking out more movement. Yes, again, the flash of steel. Now he saw the tall hat bobbing above a spur of rock.

A thrill of excitement hurried through Fallon. He had to see what lay over the ridge above him. And it had to be cattle. He'd heard them. It didn't take too much imagination to conclude he had found the rustlers' roost and the destination of the man who had shot down Cap Milton.

Ten minutes on he found his path finally blocked by a huge mass of limestone rock thrusting up spurs like the edges of rotting teeth. It commanded a perfect view of what lay beyond the ridge.

His hand shook a little as he tied the bay and allowed his gaze to search the rock face for a way up there. After a patient study he found it. The way was hazardous, but it was climbable.

He licked his lips now, which he found were suddenly dry, and rubbed his hard palms together, which were moist. He wasn't a climbing man, never had been, but he was going to have to be if he wanted to find out what was beyond that ridge.

He picked his way slowly, not looking down. Inch by inch he felt his way up, seeking cracks, crevices and toe-holds. He quickly found riding boots were not ideal for the work.

He was breathing hard by the time he reached the uneven top and had to suppress it as best he could. He found the upthrust, the dominant look-out point for miles around and it had to hold a man doing just that duty, he reasoned.

His grey stare scanned the broken rocky surface.

The last of the sun was sharding red and gold light through the gaps in the hills across the ravine west.

Then Fallon heard the cough and saw the thread of tobacco smoke trickle up from behind the rock some two dozen yards ahead of him.

He blinked and found his lips were stuck together now, as though glued. He swallowed hard on the dryness in his throat. Man, this lookout was awful sure nobody would be coming in the way he had chosen to do, he decided. Fallon passed a sinewy hand over his hard features. Well, if he was going to move, it had to be now.

He slid out his Colt, feeling his body tightening up, an aliveness spurting energy through it, his senses lifting, his wound forgotten.

He moved forward with the caution of a mountain cat.

He heard the man spit, cough again, break wind and chuckle to himself.

But Fallon was not amused. He was close enough now to hear the man's heavy breathing.

Fallon rounded the rock the owlhoot was behind swiftly. His sudden appearance caused the lookout's quirley to drop from his mouth in astonishment and his eyes to stare, startled to see the grim, big man standing over him.

Without hesitation, Fallon brought his gun crashing down on the owlhoot's tall ten gallon hat curtailing, brutally, any more movement from the alarmed watchman.

As the rustler dropped with a harsh cry, Fallon went to ground with him, his hand clamping over the watchman's mouth, before beating him over the head again as the owlhoot started to move. This time the rustler went still.

Fallon went quiet too, stilling his racing breathing. The hills were quiet again. No more sound, only more lowing of cattle from beyond the ridge. And for the first time Fallon looked down into the long, narrow, but verdant valley which seemed to move into flatter country north. It was supporting quite a large herd of beeves, too.

Maybe a mile to the north west, in the blue evening light, was a crude cabin. Yellow pricks of light showed at the windows.

Fallon felt almost sure this was the rustlers'
hideout. It had to be.

He settled back against the rock, thrilled with
his discovery. Well, there was one certain way to
find out. He shook the unconscious owlhoot until
he groaned and rolled his head.

It took Fallon some time to get the rustler fully
alert. Eventually he found himself staring into
the man's resentful brown eyes.

'Who's payin' you?' he ground out meanly when
the man was fully aroused.

Fallon saw fierce rage come to the owlhoot's
swarthy face, then he felt the man's saliva splash
on to his face.

'Go to hell!' gritted the rustler.

Taken completely by surprise, disgusted anger
flamed through Fallon. Why, the dirty, low-
gutted …

He crashed his bunched fist into the owlhoot's
bony face – once, twice, three times.

'You low-down sonofabitch,' he hissed. Again he
hit him, his whole being outraged by the rustler's
action.

The owlhoot moaned and rolled his head, but
still his stare was defiant, almost mocking, as it
turned up to Fallon as he finished his beating.

The owlhoot muttered through mashed lips. 'It's
still 'go to hell ,' he snarled.

Fallon, full of cold meanness now, hoisted his
Bowie knife. He was in no frame of mind to
humour this man. He wanted answers, and quick.

'It is, eh?' he hissed menacingly. His eyes turned to two iron-grey slits. He brought the blade up towards the man's now rounding, frightened gaze. 'I could cut your eyes out,' he snarled harshly. 'Now, that sure would be "hell" fer you, *hombre.*'

Suddenly the owlhoot's whole demeanour drastically altered. It seemed to Fallon that cold steel was a new dimension and had not been anticipated by the rustler.

'God almighty!' he breathed, cringing away. 'Careful with thet knife, mister!'

Fallon made as though he hadn't heard. He held the man's shirt in his iron-hard left fist and turned the blade in his right hand towards the man's left eye. 'Spill it,' he menaced meanly.

The owlhoot cowered back further, straining against Fallon's powerful grip, his face twisted with fear. 'Oh, God, don't, mister,' he wailed. 'All I know is ... Wade Coleman ... he gives us information where we can pick up cattle easy.'

The words came blurting out, terror now clear in the owlhoot's eyes as they looked fretfully at the Bowie knife an inch from them.

Fallon felt a warmth of satisfaction fill him. He'd hit the answer to the rustling right on the nose ... but why? Was it because Coleman just couldn't help himself?

Having no time for further speculation Fallon put away his knife and hoisted the owlhoot to his feet. He was a slight man and easy to handle.

'Where's your horse?' he rasped.

The battered owlhoot jerked his head towards the valley. 'At the foot of the spur.'

Fallon whipped off his bandana and stuffed it into the protesting, bleeding mouth of the owlhoot. He now took off the rustler's own bandana and tied it tightly across the owlhoot's mouth.

'Git down there,' he ordered nastily. 'Any tricks an' – '

Fallon hefted the Bowie again. 'This don't make a lot of noise.'

Thoroughly cowed now and seemingly glad to be alive, the owlhoot followed a well trodden path. Dark shadows were closing down on the hills and the moon was rising above the eastern hills.

The owlhoot's horse was a stocky, unkempt mustang. Fallon motioned to the rustler to take the reins, his hand clamped on to the man's shirt at the nape of his neck, then he turned the *hombre* towards where his own bay was tethered.

Within ten minutes, walking in full dark now, they reached it.

Fallon tied the man's hands to the saddle horn and removed the gag before he ordered, 'Walk your horse down the hill.'

'Where you takin' me?' quavered the owlhoot.

'Where you have to sing for your supper.'

TEN

Soon after noon the following day Fallon eased his tired bay up the long valley towards the High Baldy ranchhouse.

A few yards ahead of him the owlhoot rode his mustang, his bruised head nodding on to his chest, his hands still tied in front of him.

Fallon had pressed on relentlessly, ignoring the rustler's pleas for rest. An urgent impatience hustled inside Fallon. Before very long he could have Coleman where he belonged, either dead or jailed.

It gave him a stern satisfaction to dwell on that. Little had he dreamed, when he had involved himself in the killing at Tonto Springs, that it would have led to this. He had long since reluctantly come to terms with the fact that he would have to be satisfied with the punishment already meted out to Coleman. After all, though he had been gut-sure Coleman had had his father killed, Fallon had to accept there had remained the element of doubt.

But now ...

Mace Readon and maybe six hands were standing in front of the ranchhouse when he rode into the bare area before it.

The rancher stepped forward, his gaunt, leathery face grim. He eyed the owlhoot narrowly before returning his questioning gaze to Fallon.

Fallon dismounted and hauled the rustler unceremoniously out of the saddle to leave him collapsed on the ground, groaning.

Readon looked hard at the owlhoot before returning his gaze to Fallon and saying, with warning in his voice, 'Mat … do you know you've got a posse of twenty men out searchin' for you? Talk is you shot down Cap Milton.' The rancher's eyes narrowed. 'Thet right?'

Fallon turned grey eyes on to Readon's weathered, inquiring face.

'No, Mace,' he said evenly, 'it ain't. I found Cap shot to bits on the trail.'

Fallon went on to tell the full story.

When he'd finished, Mace Readon seemed to believe him. 'Well, I sorta figured you had more savvy than to do damned-fool thing like that,' he growled. Now the rancher turned his blue gaze on to the rustler.

'Who's this?'

Fallon spat through the dust riming his lips. 'One of the boys who's been pickin' at your herd, an' I know where they're holed up.'

Readon squinted against the harsh light of the sun, his look hardening. 'The hell you say,' he breathed.

His face grim, the rancher bent and hauled the battered owlhoot to his feet and stared at his bloody and bruised face.

'Seems you've been havin' more than words with this *hombre*, Fallon,' he said with a grim smile splitting his thin lips. 'Get anythin' out of the sonofabitch?'

'Coleman's passin' on information.'

Mace Readon's eyes widened, and Fallon watched satisfaction filling them. 'I knew it,' the rancher muttered. 'He's allus askin' about where I was movin' my cattle and why. Says he wants to learn as much about ranchin' as he can. That gut-low sonofabitch.'

Rage clear in him now, Readon shook the owlhoot and stared hard at him. 'Damn you, you stealin' varmint! Where's my beef?'

Fallon stepped forward. 'Let him go, Mace. Leave him to me.'

The angry rancher complied reluctantly and Fallon stared at the tired, dejected owlhoot.

'How many men you got?'

A glimmer of defiance now came to the owlhoot's eyes. 'I ain't tellin',' he muttered through swollen lips. He looked with some pleading in his eyes at the rangemen standing narrow-eyed around him, as if hoping for some sign of succour.

With a violent snatch Fallon hauled him round, bringing his big Bowie up as he did so.

Again, he steered the vicious-looking blade to within half an inch of the owlhoot's alarmed stare.

'We've bin over this ground before, mister,' Fallon menaced. 'Patience ain't my strong point.'

'You won't use it,' challenged the owlhoot. His eyes reached again towards the hard-eyed rangemen. 'Especially with witnesses here.'

Fallon wrapped his big left hand through the owlhoot's long, matted, dark hair, jerking his head back, and pressed the blade on to the man's jugular. 'I said you had to do some singin'.'

The rustler gave out a harsh cry, still striving to look pleadingly at the cowmen, but found no comfort.

'Fifteen!' he shouted then, sudden panic in his voice, his nerves obviously in shreds.

'Who had the sheriff shot?' Fallon demanded harshly.

'Cap Milton dead?' The owlhoot looked fearful. 'Hell, I know nothin' about thet. Nothin' at all.'

Fallon was relentless. He jerked the man's head back further until he was struggling for balance. 'Whoever it was,' Fallon growled nastily, 'headed straight for your camp. You had to see somethin'.'

The owlhoot's eyes were terrified orbs now as he met Fallon's bleak stare. 'I saw Coleman ridin' in an hour afore you showed, is all …'

Fallon stared with disbelief at the rustler, before his harsh voice cut across the owlhoot's reply. 'Coleman?'

'Yeah.' The rustler's gaze again turned to pleading. 'He was the only one I saw enter camp from the Greenville direction.'

'That ain't the Coleman I knew,' Fallon said to

nobody in particular. 'He always had his killin' done for him.'

He let the owlhoot drop to the ground and the rustler lay groaning there.

'If he has done the killin', though,' he said, 'we have him.' He looked at Readon. 'Mace, how long to get your boys together?'

The rancher's grim face lengthened. 'An hour.' His eyes searched the weary lines on Fallon's face. 'Meanwhile, you look as though you could do with a meal.'

Fallon rasped his beard. He *was* tired, hungry and dirty, and his wound was throbbing. He nodded. 'Well, I won't argue with that. Will your cook fix me up?'

'I'll see to it,' Readon said briskly. 'Meanwhile, clean up.' He cast his keen blue gaze towards Fallon's bay now. 'You need a fresh horse, too. The mare looks all in.'

Fallon was grateful for Readon's hospitality and his readiness to accept his words. He turned towards the long trough leading away from the wind pump and pulled off his shirt, inspecting the stitches in his side as he did so. The wound looked free from infection and was healing well. He'd have to see the doc about the stitches …

Fallon was washed, shaved and fed by the time the High Baldy riders were assembled. Fourteen hard-visaged men with liberal hardware and an obvious inclination to use it, if necessary. It was clear none of the rangeman took rustling lightly.

The owlhoot had been fed, too, and allowed to clean up. Now he was sitting tied to the verandah rail.

Readon had picked out a frisky roan for Fallon and Fallon now had his saddle on its back. Then he had watered the bay and turned her into the corral, leaving her to chew on the corn and sweet hay put out for her.

It was then one of the hands grunted, 'Riders.' He pointed towards the southern end of the valley.

Readon frowned and looked questioningly at Fallon, who was equally puzzled. The rancher took a hunting telescope out of his large coat pocket. It was in a leather case. Soon he had it to his right eye. When he took it away, his look was serious as it met Fallon's grey stare.

'It's the posse,' the rancher said tensely.

Fallon clamped his wide lips together. 'Damn it!' he growled.

He fished around his now fast-working brain to find some way out of this complication. The posse would want to take him to Greenville, of that he had no doubt. They would want to put him on trial. And he doubted if they would listen to any speculation about it being Coleman who had done the shooting first off; even if he told them he had trailed the saloon owner to the rustlers' roost, and even if the owlhoot corroborated his suspicions. Coleman could well talk his way out of it, aided by the evidence of the man who had found him by the sheriff's body. Fallon decided he couldn't risk that.

He wanted – no – needed, to get to Coleman first.
To get him on his own. He needed to do it his way.

'I ain't goin' to wait to argue with them, Mace,'
he said. 'Look, could you get the Lazy M riders to
side you?'

Readon nodded vigorously. 'I'm sure,' he said
firmly. 'Their trouble is our trouble and vice versa.
Allus has been.'

Fallon nodded. 'Well, I tell you – that valley the
owlhoots are in ... it's a mini fortress they've got
up there. But, maybe, if you know it, you know of
a way in that ain't so hard ...'

He went on to describe the country he had
ridden through to find the owlhoots' lair and the
apparent easier outlet of the valley he had seen
going to the north.

'That's got to be Lonesome Valley,' Readon cut
in before Fallon had finished. 'It's too high to be of
all-year-round use. The winters have beaten three
men who have tried to settle it, to my own
knowledge. Ain't been bothered with for years
now.' He laughed ironically. 'Well, damn me ...
Lonesome Valley. Who'd have thought it?'

Fallon said, 'You can take the owlhoot for good
measure. He sings quite well with a little
persuasion.'

Readon nodded, became serious and studied
Fallon's gaunt features. 'What do you aim to do,
Mat?'

'I figure to pay Coleman a visit.'

Readon's blue eyes narrowed. 'That won't be
easy and could be dangerous.'

Fallon turned and climbed on to the back of the frisky roan. Astride he looked down at the lanky rancher.

'No, it won't be easy, and yes, it will be dangerous, but if you root out the rustlers and get a few birds to sing,' he suggested, 'I figure to stop that *hombre* if he smells we're on to him and decides to run.'

Fallon turned to look at the posse now coming down the lush valley in a tight bunch. They were moving slowly, as if tired, and were still maybe a couple of miles away.

'Turn them off me if you can, Mace,' he requested. 'And maybe, in a day or two, all our troubles will be over.'

With that he swung the roan and headed west.

ELEVEN

Fallon looked down into the wide, shallow depression in the range that held Greenville. Lights were sprinkled throughout the town, looking like glow-worms in the night. The pain from his wound was a mixture of itchy irritation and soreness, which he bore with impatience.

He had waited for dark, catching a couple of hours' sleep while he did. But in doing so he had found, if anything, it had made him feel more tired. He knew the feeling would pass, though, and he would feel the benefit of it later.

He urged his roan down the gradual slope now, openly riding. He reckoned if he moved towards town furtively, despite the dark, it would maybe arouse suspicion in somebody. And with the ruthless shooting down of Sheriff Cap Milton, trigger-fingers would be itchy – especially where the law was concerned, which he felt must have some representation in town, despite the posse.

He knew the position of the High Stake Saloon and made for the rear entrance, only to have disappointment fill him.

There wasn't one.

He licked his lips, cursing quietly under his breath. In the dark, helped by the light of the moon, his gaze began to search the warping boards that composed the rear wall of the saloon and gaming-house until it found the sash window. The room it belonged to was in darkness.

He dismounted and led the roan to a tie-rail some thirty yards from the rear of the High Stake. There, it would attract less attention.

Then he paused for moments while he listened, allowing his gaze to search the area for any movement. When he had satisfied himself he was alone he moved quickly to the sash window and thrust the blade of his Bowie in the gap. He found it easy to slip the catch, the window being a loose fit.

He eased it open cautiously and climbed inside, immediately drawing it down behind him. He paused once more, his keened-up hearing listening for any noises of movement.

Only the usual familiar sounds of a saloon in full swing came. The tinkling piano, the raucous laughter, the clash of glasses, the click of roulette wheels.

He felt a bead of sweat run from under his stetson. He ignored it. Narrow-eyed, he slid out his Colt.

He was in some sort of store-room. He could see bulky packages, cleaning utensils – silver in the light from the moon angling in through the window.

His gaze found the door now and he tiptoed towards it. He tried the latch. The door cracked open. Outside was a corridor, dimly lit by two oil lamps in brackets on the far wall.

It was deserted.

He swung the door open fully and stepped out, pulling the door to again behind him. There were three doors in the passageway. Irritation scurried through him. Damn it! It was a complication he could have done without.

He opened the first. There was no light from the chink at the bottom of the door. But the woman was white-faced and round-eyed in the pale light from the oil lamps in the corridor, lying on the bed under the strenuously-working man on top of her.

Fallon hastily apologised and retreated, closing the door again quietly. But the discovery momentarily intrigued him. Coleman ran a brothel, too?

The third door had light coming through the gaps in it. This time he was more cautious.

There were voices coming from inside. He recognised the tone of the one now speaking to be Coleman's.

'For God's sake, leave it, Will,' he was saying irritably. 'Cap Milton had things on us, I'm sure of it. And when I saw him riding Fallon out of town, Fallon knowing what he does, I couldn't take the chance. I had to use the opportunity.'

'What does Fallon know?' came an equally irate voice in answer. 'You're only guessing. It was a crazy thing to do to kill the sheriff. Sometimes, Wade, I just don't understand you.'

'Last time I left too many bastards with mouths to give evidence,' Coleman growled. 'This time, there will be no mistakes.'

'Damn it,' the other voice came back, 'can't you see? This is the biggest mistake you ever made, Wade. When Milton came to see you the day before yesterday he was fishing. Pushing you. He knew nothing.'

'I knew, as soon as he wanted to know what Brink here, and Chance were doing in my hotel and visiting me, he was on to us,' Coleman said, clearly worried.

'Names on posters! Nothing concrete!'

'Nevertheless …' Coleman's voice trailed off for moments. Fallon heard the saloon owner make an annoyed growl now. 'Anyway, what the hell are you going on about, Will?' he demanded. 'They're blaming Fallon for it, aren't they? Just like I said they would. And Wally Jason, finding Fallon bending over the sheriff like he did was an extra bonus for us. They have a posse out combing the hills for Fallon right now. And when they catch him, they'll sure as hell string him up.'

To Fallon's surprise, he heard Brink Mather's harsh voice cut in now. 'I wanted Fallon,' he snorted.

Coleman still sounded argumentative. 'Leave it to the posse, Brink,' he ordered harshly. 'He'll get what's coming. What is more to the point – what's this about a man going missing at the hideout?'

'It was discovered after you left last night,' Mather answered curtly.

'Has he run out?'

'Not Peeson. He wouldn't run out on the type of deal we got goin'.'

'You sound damn sure,' Coleman snorted.

'Sure enough,' returned Mather. 'I know the man from way back.'

Again, there was a pause. Fallon pressed closer to the door.

'Then somebody must have him,' came Coleman's voice now. 'Someone has found the hideout.'

'I told you it was crazy to get involved with the rustling!' the man named Will cut in worriedly.

Coleman made a disparaging noise. 'They've nothing on me. Nothing at all. You know that as well as I do, Will.'

'Men talk, Wade!'

Again there was silence, then Coleman said urgently,

'Brink? What do you figure?'

'I don't think that pack you've got up there are reliable,' Mather said, criticism in his voice.

Fallon heard boots pacing the floor now. 'But … only you, Chance, Rafe Collins and Bert Weston know about me,' Coleman's voice argued. 'The rest know nothing.'

'I've found Weston drinks too much,' countered Brink, 'and when he does his tongue gets loose. I tell you, Wade, the whole pack up there know about you and I'd trust them about as much as I'd trust a coyote.'

'I knew it!' wailed Will. 'We're done for, Wade.'

Then Fallon felt the door give before his pressed

body, as he strained to hear as much as he could. As it did, startled anxiety raged through him. He stumbled into the room.

Brink Mather was lounging in a leather chair to the left of the door, now staring up. A small, dour-looking man was sitting in the corner directly ahead of Fallon and to the right, his owlish eyes round and startled. Coleman was pacing the floor in front of an expensive mahogany desk.

A desperate snarl immediately came from Mather. As soon as he saw it was Fallon, he was going snake-fast for his Colt.

Fallon swung, dropping into a gunfighter's crouch. His first shot took Brink in the chest, just above the heart, the second hit the navel, sending him screaming and writhing to the ground, his lead pumping into the floor.

Fallon turned his gun now on Coleman, but was distracted by the man in the far corner of the office. He was pulling a small revolver from a shoulder holster.

Though realising that van Klieber was the immediate danger, anxiously, Fallon saw Coleman was heading for the window. He wanted him. By God, he wanted him!

But Coleman was crashing through glass when Fallon sent his first load towards the little man, hoping to dispense with the threat as quickly as possible.

Van Klieber was starting to shoot as Fallon saw his first bullet hit the small man in the shoulder, spinning him out of his chair. Van Klieber now started to go crab-wise across the floor, moaning, his gun falling to the boards.

Knowing he was out of the fight, Fallon swiftly replaced the loads he had discharged from his Colt.

Then he went out through the window after Coleman.

TWELVE

Coleman hit the ground amid a shower of wood and glass. He was amazed to find he had got away with only a few minor cuts to his hands and face. As he came to his feet, he heard further gunfire in the office.

Not waiting for the outcome he ran off up the alley, panic rampant in him. He could not even guess how Fallon had found him, or how he came to be here, in Greenville. But suddenly, everything was going wrong. Yesterday, he had been talking with Jane. He had been making plans for the wedding. He had even been talking about running for governor next election time.

Now ...

He ran blindly, alarm defeating any further constructive thought, before, disgusted with himself, he halted his frightened run. So complete had been his initial consternation he was surprised to find his bolt had taken him half a mile, to the north end of the town, near the outskirts.

He wiped his brow with a shaky hand. He had

to think, be rational. He had to deal a way around these setbacks. So things had gone slightly wrong. If, as Brink Mather had said, the whole gang knew he was involved, albeit covertly, there was still time to get to the hideout, pay the men off and tell them to scatter. Thinking back, he now reckoned it had been a mistake to go to the hideout yesterday. His appearance would have been bound to have caused more speculation. But he had just wanted to warn them to lie low while the posse was out – be on the lookout for trouble.

Now, as van Klieber had warned him on numerous occasions, his impatience had thwarted him again. Again he had tried to run a bit too fast. Maybe he was too ambitious. Van Klieber had always tried to throw a loop on him. Slow him down.

He halted his nagging thoughts. What had happened to his one true friend? Was he dead? The concern he felt was almost a total stranger to him. People in the past had just been tools he used. But Will van Klieber ... well, Will had been something else.

He saw Thompson's livery ahead now and reckoned Sandy Bowen, the hostler, would still be up. Now that he had calmed and he was thinking logically again a plan came swiftly to mind. And he decided it could just work.

He stepped into the dark, cavernous stables. Horses moved restlessly in their stalls as he entered. He knew Sandy had a little office off to the left. Coleman could see the light there and

Sandy sat on a box, half-bottle of whisky on the makeshift table before him. He was reading.

'Want to earn five dollars, Sandy?' he said.

Coleman could see he had startled the hostler.

'Why ... Mr Coleman.' The greying livery hand looked up at him, round-eyed.

Coleman knew he had gained a high degree of respect in the town and was not often seem in such lowly places, getting boys or barmen to fetch his horses when he wanted them.

'Five dollars?' the hostler was saying now, quickly getting over his surprise. He grinned. 'Damn it, I'd jump over the moon fer thet.'

Coleman smiled his most disarming smile. 'Well, no need to go as far as that, Sandy. I just want you to take a message.'

'To do with the shootin' I heard?' the hostler probed now, alertly.

Coleman nodded soberly, his face full of hollows in the lamp light. 'A terrible business,' he supplied, 'from which I have been lucky to escape with my life. An acquaintance of mine, and Mr van Klieber, have been cold-bloodedly shot down – and in my own office –'

'Mr van Klieber?' Sandy interrupted aghast. 'God almighty. Now, who'd want to do that to a gentleman like him?'

'The man who did it was trying to get at me,' Coleman went on with drama in his voice. 'He's already shot down Sheriff Milton in cold blood.'

'Not this Fallon *hombre* the posse are after?' asked Sandy incredulously.

Coleman nodded grimly. 'The same. He has a grudge against me, too, it seems, and he doesn't care who he kills to get at me.'

The hostler licked his lips and stood up briskly, hitching up his tobacco-brown corduroy trousers. 'Well, what is it you want me to do, Mr Coleman?' he demanded. 'Though I hope you ain't askin' me to go up agin him.'

Coleman, slightly surprised by the suggestion, for the man must be at least sixty, looked at the hostler's serious face.

'No, nothing like that, Sandy,' he assured. 'I just want you to go to the sheriff's office and tell the duty deputy Fallon is on the streets and gunning for me. I'd go myself, but I have no gun – never carried a sidearm in my life. Frankly, I feel if I go back on the streets now I would be in mortal danger.'

Sandy pulled on a shabby hat. He appeared proud to be of service. 'Ain't no need to pay me fer doin' thet, Mr Coleman,' he said. 'It's my bounden duty as a citizen.'

'I know,' said Coleman smoothly. 'But I've disturbed your reading, and there is a killer roaming the streets – though I don't think he'll bother you ... I just feel I should give you something.'

Sandy nodded. 'Well, the money sure would come in useful, I won't deny it. But I don't want it known I'd take pay to do my duty as a citizen.'

'And nobody will know, Sandy,' Coleman

assured silkily. He pressed the notes into the hostler's hand. 'Now get to it.'

Coleman waited then, after he had seen Sandy heading down the street towards the sheriff's office. Waited until he heard the sounds of men's voices; waited for the groups of armed townspeople, outraged by the news, to get on to the streets.

Now he moved with careful furtiveness. He saddled the big chestnut stallion he stalled here and led it down the back streets towards his office again. Once he came face to face with a group of armed and angry men. He knew the man in the lead to be Saul Freely, the haberdasher.

'Mr Coleman,' he said. 'You should be off the streets. Leave us to deal with this Fallon *hombre*.'

Coleman knew it was well known in the town that he never carried a sidearm, and only carried a rifle when he left town. And his supposed aversion to violence was respected.

'Though it goes against the grain, men,' he said, 'I think I should get my rifle and do what I can.'

Freely nodded. 'As you wish, Mr Coleman,' he said. 'But there's no need.'

Coleman smiled. 'I thank you for your consideration,' he said. 'But I feel I must take a part in this manhunt. After all, it is me he is after and he has shot down my dear friend Will van Klieber.'

'Well, I'm happy to tell you he'll be okay,' assured Freely. 'He's at Doc Somer's now. Took lead in the shoulder. Though the other man in the office is dead.'

Coleman shook his dark, still handsome head, his lips set grim. 'He must be found, this killer,' he said with feeling. 'He must be dealt with.' He put warning in his look now. 'Don't dally with him, men. When you're sure you've sighted him, shoot him down before more good men are killed.'

Freely's lean, hard face was serious in the light from the lanterns the men carried on sticks.

'We'll get him, Mr Coleman,' he said, 'never fear. If he's still in town, we'll get him.'

Coleman nodded. 'Well, that's comforting to hear. Now, if you don't mind, I'll get my rifle and join you as soon as I can.'

Coleman entered his office through the broken window. He felt it better to keep in the background as much as he could.

Inside, all that remained of Brink Mather and van Klieber were bloodstains on the good carpets.

Coleman ignored them. Instead, he emptied the safe of its contents, stocks, coin and notes, packing them into the saddlebags he had with him.

He had to get to the men in the hills. He had to pay them off. He had to get rid of their damning influence, then lie low, marry Jane and ...

He blinked in the silver light of the moon coming in through the broken window behind him. But, if the posse had got to the owlhoots first and they had started to sing, well ... He had the monies in his saddlebags, wealth in other banks, accounts under other names. And he could send for William van Klieber discreetly, when the dust had settled ...

But if the posse hadn't got to the owlhoots, then,

when he had dispersed them and the evidence they could give, he would have control of the Lazy M and the oil he knew was under it.

He took his rifle out of the gun rack next to the window, plus a pocket full of shells before stepping out of the window and into the alley.

THIRTEEN

Fallon felt satisfaction fill him when he saw Coleman come out of the night. His hunch had proved right.

From where he lay, on the roof of the building next to the rear of the High Stake Saloon, he'd observed Coleman tie up his horse and enter his office through the broken window. Five minutes later Fallon had watched the saloon owner climb out again, clutching two bulky saddlebags.

The hunch had come to Fallon as he left the High Stake office through the broken window. An instinct had warned him not to chase Coleman, but to wait. So there he had lain on the roof, watched them carry away Brink Mather and the small, game *hombre*, who was still apparently alive.

And also, while he had waited, and minutes before Coleman had shown up, Fallon had listened to a group of armed townspeople who had paused below his hideout.

'He's lit out,' one had said. 'He wouldn't be hangin' around after what he's done.'

'Yup,' said another. 'Reckon we ought to be formin' a posse.'

'Hell, there's already one out lookin' for him,' the first returned. 'Damn it, he's got gall.'

Fallon had felt a worm of anxiety when another said, staring at Fallon's mount up the alley, 'Know who owns the roan tied up there?'

Nobody knew, but the consensus of opinion was it couldn't be Fallon's for he'd be long gone and wouldn't be so dumb-witted to do a damn-fool thing like that, anyway.

So they had moved away and Fallon had exhaled thankfully.

Now, to his slight surprise, Coleman led his horse up the alley, making for the south side of town, the closest to the open range. He seemed to be making no effort to seek the help of the townspeople, or to assist in their search. And Fallon thought: damn it, he's cutting and running ...

With lithe movements he dropped off the roof, got his roan and followed the saloon owner discreetly. The noise made by the searching townspeople seemed to be coming from the north-west of town, away from them.

He passed two people, who ignored him and went hurrying off up a side alley to one of the main streets, carrying rifles.

He mounted when he reached the open range, ensuring first that Coleman could not observe him.

Now Fallon's whole body tensed up. A cold,

deadly purpose filled him. He felt sure he had the sonofabitch; felt sure he had the man who, he was certain, had ordered the death of his father. Soon he felt a debt, long-standing, would be paid.

A mile out on the moon-silvered range, Fallon watched the dark shape of Coleman and his horse swing north. Immediately, Fallon's hard visage grew even more grim and the move gave him food for thought – very serious calculation.

After swift deliberation he urged the roan into a long gallop, swinging wide to the west. He must get in front of Coleman, for he now had the strong hunch the saloon owner was heading for the owlhoot lair. All the logic he could muster pointed to it.

An hour later he pulled rein in a scatter of rocks and waited.

Sure enough, to his deep satisfaction, Coleman showed and Fallon put his roan out across his path, his Colt lined up on the saloon owner.

'Hold it, you mangy sonofabitch!' he ordered.

An almost animal snarl came from Coleman as his dark eyes peered through the moon-silvered space between them.

'Fallon!' he snarled, his face an evil mask. 'Damn your hide. You've dogged my trail long enough.'

Fallon was surprised to see Coleman unsuccessfully fumble for his rifle in its boot at his thigh.

'Pull it and I'll shoot you down like a dog!' Fallon warned harshly.

But, to his amazement, Coleman appeared not

to heed him. Instead, after failing to draw his rifle, he dug spurs into his big chestnut stallion and sent it cannoning forward into Fallon's roan, sending the beast staggering.

Then Coleman put his nostril-flared and wild-eyed animal into a flat-out run past Fallon while still wrestling to free his rifle.

Fallon gathered his startled roan and swung her into a gallop after the hard-riding saloon owner, cursing his bad management of the attempted arrest.

The trail, he soon found, was rugged. Rocks freely sprinkled it and Fallon had to ease down his mount, fearful she might break a leg, or worse. But Coleman appeared to have no such qualms, or was driven by fear.

His stallion was whistling shrilly in the night as Coleman crouched forward in the saddle, urging it with vicious spur rakes along its flanks.

Then it happened, as Fallon suspected it might. Agonised squealing came from the chestnut and he could see it lunging forward, crashing through the rocks and trail-side rubble, sending Coleman flying forward. The saloon owner hit an outcrop with bone-crushing force. His anguished cry seemed to cut off mid-voice, as though extinguished by a garotte.

Fallon dismounted by his side. Coleman was lying, his body twisted, staring up at him, his dark eyes wild, but dead. The violence of his fall had snapped his neck. Fallon could see the spine poking through the flesh, blood welling out.

Eyes narrow and grim-faced, Fallon now turned his attention to the stallion threshing in the night. It was attempting to get up, but its right fore cannon was snapped and flapping about. The handsome beast was squealing its agony as it attempted to use it. It toppled again and this time it lay, its eyes wild, rolling up and looking at him.

There was only one thing for it. Regretfully, Fallon reached for his rifle.

FOURTEEN

Fallon learned the Lazy M and the High Baldy had combined and had taken the owlhoot lair completely by surpise, coming in through the almost unguarded northern pass into the valley.

Bit by bit the machinations of Coleman's deceits had been uncovered and confessed, and van Klieber had been coerced into making a contribution, also confirming Coleman shot down Sheriff Milton. And, to Fallon's mild surprise, Chance Mather had met him and made his peace.

Fallon had said his farewells to Mace Readon and the High Baldy boys and was now sitting his saddle before the long verandah of the Lazy M ranchhouse looking down at Jane Marsden's pale, dark-eyed face.

'Ma'am, though I hated Coleman, it don't give me any high pleasure to be proved right an' see you unhappy,' he said. 'You've had grief enough.'

She nodded, her hair sleek as raven wings in the sun. 'You're a good man, Mat,' she said, 'and I'm sure it doesn't.' Her sad stare hardened, even though her lower lip quivered and she dropped

her head for a moment. 'Wade certainly took me
for a fool,' she added bitterly.

Fallon nodded, feeling oddly clumsy and having
to fish for the right words. 'I guess you ain't the
only one he's done that to, ma'am,' he said quietly.
'He had a silken tongue.'

Now Fallon touched his hat with a horny finger.

'Well, Jane,' he said, with a faint feeling of
regret, 'I guess it's got to be goodbye.'

He was surprised to see Jane's eyes turn up
swiftly and meet his grey stare, a hint of pleading
in them.

'I could still use a top hand, Mat,' she said
quickly. 'And you more than fill the bill.'

Fallon felt mild surprise, even delight invade
him. For a moment he was almost sure he could
read something more in Jane Marsden's eyes,
too ...

The hard, grim lines he had worn ever since he
had come to this range softened. 'Why, Jane,' he
said warmly. 'I ain't had a better offer than that
all day.'

He added, crow's-feet growing at the corners of
his eyes, 'An' maybe, in a little while, when ...'

He squinted his eyes shyly and shoved his hat
to the back of his head. 'Well, what I'm tryin' to
say is, ma'am – I ain't sparked a gal fer quite a
spell. And you, Jane Marsden, more than fill the
bill in thet direction.'

To his surprise, Jane smiled happily. 'Why, Mat
Fallon – I never thought you had it in you ...'

Fallon arched his brows and gave her a long

look before he thought, come to think of it, Jane,
neither did I until this moment. And he turned his
bay mare towards the bunkhouse of the Lazy M,
whistling softly.